# A Frightening Discovery

Randal opened the door and stepped into his room—only to come to a sudden halt on the other side of the threshold.

Magic! But this magic was strange, like nothing he had known before. Randal looked around the room, which was lit by an eerie, blue-white glow.

"Wizard . . ."

The faint whisper came from his bed, over in the corner. Randal looked and saw a man lying there, his features drawn and ashen in the cold blue light. Randal forced himself to go over to the cot and grasp the man by the shoulder.

The young wizard pulled his hand back quickly. *He's dying*, he realized. *He's dying of magic.*

# CIRCLE OF MAGIC

# THE WIZARD'S STATUE

Debra Doyle and James D. Macdonald

illustrated by Judith Mitchell

Troll

*To the Siren of Seal Beach, who sang to us while
we were stranded on a foreign shore—
and read our manuscripts, too.*

This edition published in 2003.

Originally published under the title *Circle of Magic: City by the Sea.*

Copyright © 1990 by Troll Communications L.L.C.

Cover photography by Steven Dolce.

~~in~~ Canada.

6  5

# I.

# Old Friends Meeting

RANDAL OF DOUN, a sturdy brown-haired youth of about fifteen, pulled up the hood of his dark robe and hurried through the narrow streets of the Woodworkers' District. Here in Cingestoun the afternoons were cool, even though the season was not yet autumn. The River Donchess flowed through the middle of town, and the wind brought damp air off the water.

He paused at the corner and looked quickly up the next street. A man he'd spoken with earlier had told him that Alured Carpenter had a helper named Nicolas. That could mean only one thing: Randal's friend Nick, from the Schola Sorceriae—the School of Wizardry in Tarnsberg—was still working here.

In the old days, when Randal had despaired of completing his own apprenticeship, Nick's help and advice had sometimes been the only things that kept him going. But in the middle of Randal's second year, Nick had startled everybody by leaving both the Schola and the practice of wizardry. Nick had traveled north, to Cingestoun, to work in a carpenter's shop.

This street, Carpenters' Lane, was the place. Randal looked into the open front of each shop as he came to it. Then, at last, Randal spotted his friend—a young man with a curly brown beard, leather-aproned, with a hammer in his hand and a trickle of sweat rolling down his forehead.

"Nick!" Randal shouted.

The young man looked up. "Who . . . Randy!" The journeyman carpenter put down his hammer and hurried to the front of the shop. "Come in, come in. I never expected to see you again after I left Tarnsberg, but I should have known someday you'd come walking in the door!"

Nick clasped Randal around the shoulders, nearly squeezing the life out of him with a friendly bear hug. "Let me take a look at you." Nick stepped back and gave Randal an appraising glance. "And wearing a journeyman's robes, too. So you made it. I knew that no one would ever beat my record as the apprentice wizard who went the longest without becoming a journeyman."

He steered Randal inside the shop and over to a bench. "Sit down and tell me the news. Cingestoun may be a big town, but not much word from the outside world comes through the gates."

Randal sat, accepted the cool drink that Nick offered, and began to tell what he'd seen and heard on the road. "Times are hard," he said. "Crops are failing from one side of Brecelande to the other, and robbers are everywhere."

"Then nothing much has changed since I last left the city," Nick said. "Now, tell me the news from Tarnsberg. Whatever happened to Lys? Is she still playing the lute and singing at the Grinning Gryphon Inn?"

"You can see for yourself," Randal replied. "We've been traveling together, and she's here in Cingestoun, singing at the Green Bough."

Nick's face lit up. "She is? That's wonderful! I have to watch the shop tonight for Alured, but tomorrow, I promise you, I'll stop by and see her again."

Randal smiled. Lys and Nick were his two best friends from his days in Tarnsberg. In fact, aside from his cousin Walter, who'd shared Randal's boyhood at Castle Doun, they were the best friends he had in the world.

"And how is everyone at the Schola?" Nick asked. "Mistress Pullen and all the rest?"

"Well enough," Randal replied. "Pieter's a master now."

"That's good news," said Nick. The former apprentice looked wistful for a moment. "Sometimes I wonder what might have happened if I'd stayed . . . but never mind the might-have-beens. Tell me what's become of Master Laerg—head of the Regents and running the whole Schola by now, I shouldn't wonder."

Randal looked down, suddenly unable to speak. He flexed his right hand, where a raised scar ran across the palm.

"No," Randal said quietly. "No, Master Laerg doesn't run the Schola."

He looked up, directly into Nick's eyes. "You might as well hear it all," he said. "Master Laerg is dead, and I killed him. With a sword."

"You what?" Nick asked in disbelief. Of all the laws and traditions binding wizards, the rule against using steel for attack or defense was the oldest and most revered.

Randal looked down at his lap. "I didn't have a choice," he said. "Laerg was summoning up demons . . . he wanted to destroy the Schola, and then rule all of Brecelande with the demons' help. He'd promised them a sacrifice and I was it."

"But to use a sword . . ."

Randal clenched his fist. The scar ached with the movement, as it always did—a reminder of the choice he'd made, when he'd cut himself to the bone grasping the blade of Laerg's ceremonial sword.

"I paid for it," Randal said quietly. "The Regents made me give my sworn word not to use magic until I'd gone on a quest for forgiveness to Master Balpesh off in the eastern mountains. But Balpesh let me use magic again, and taught me a few things, as well. And since then I've been living as a journeyman in truth, traveling up and down the land and seeking more magic than the Schola could teach me."

He looked about the carpenter's shop. "But what about you?" he asked Nick. "Do you use any magic at all, now that you've left the Schola?"

Nick shook his head. "I asked the Regents to put a binding spell on me," he said. "There's nothing worse than a half-taught wizard. Better to be an honest carpenter and save myself the temptation."

The street out front was dark now, and shadows filled the corners of the shop. "I have to get back,"

Randal said. "I was in the university library all day, and Lys will be wondering where I am."

Nick stood up and saw Randal to the door. "Better be careful, Randy. Cingestoun gets rough after dark."

Randal paused on the threshold, his wizard's robes swirling around him, and looked back at his friend.

"Don't worry, Nick. I'll be all right."

Nick shook his head. "This isn't Tarnsberg, remember? A black gown isn't going to keep you out of trouble—not when you've got people here who don't know a journeyman wizard from a stable hand."

"I've been a stable hand, too, and I'm not exactly helpless," Randal pointed out. "I sat through Master Issen's lectures on magical self-defense, just like everybody else."

"Of course you did," said Nick. "But as far as some people can see, you're still a half-grown boy, and a shock spell won't do a bit of good after somebody's hit you over the head from behind with a club."

Randal laughed. "For what—five copper pennies and a book of spells?"

"For the boots on your feet," Nick told him. "Like you said, times have been bad, and this year isn't any better. People are looking out for themselves."

"I know," said Randal, his laughter dying. "I told you about some of the things that are happening up around Tattinham—the robbers and bandits—but I didn't think I'd be seeing it here on the King's Road, right in the middle of Brecelande."

"It's everywhere," said Nick. "So don't get so involved in working out spells in your head that you forget to keep an eye out for trouble."

"I won't," Randal promised his friend. "I'll see you tomorrow, then."

"Until tomorrow."

The door of the carpenter's shop swung shut, leaving Randal alone in the dark. He took a firmer grasp on the tall walking staff he carried and turned down the street.

The waning moon shone down on Randal as he made his way through Cingestoun's narrow alleys to the inn where he was staying. In spite of his words to Nicolas, he wasn't particularly worried. Randal still had the strength and quick reflexes developed by his boyhood training as a squire in his uncle's castle of Doun. Although he would never use a sword again, as a journeyman wizard he had other defenses at his command.

His mind still dwelling on days past, he turned down Hornpipers' Street and entered the Green Bough, the inn where he was staying. He paused in the common room, where a clear alto voice came to him over the murmur of the crowd of patrons:

> "I wish the wind would never cease,
> Nor waters in the flood,
> 'Til all my sons come home to me
> In earthly flesh and blood."

He waved to the performer, a slender, black-haired girl dressed in boy's clothing. She sat on a

10

makeshift stage at the other end of the room and played a lute as she sang. She nodded to him, and kept on playing without losing a beat.

Randal took a seat at the back of the room and listened. Lys was a lute-player, singer, and acrobat, a native of Occitania in the far south. She made her own way as best she could with her voice and lute.

Her song done, she came across the room and took a seat by Randal. "How did your day go?" she asked.

"Fine," he said. "The university here didn't mind a journeyman wizard poking around in their library. I didn't find anything magical in there, but you never know with old books. But guess what? I found Nick! He's doing just fine at a carpenter's shop. He said he'd come by here tomorrow."

Lys smiled. "That's marvelous! If he hadn't loaned me that lute of his when I was starving, I wouldn't be able to earn my living now. I still have to sing one more time tonight—will you stay?"

"No, it's been a long day already. I think I'll go up and turn in early."

"I'll see you in the morning, then," she said.

"In the morning," Randal replied, standing up. Leaving the lute-player behind, he headed across the crowded common room toward the stairs.

The innkeeper met him at the foot of the staircase. "A word with you, wizard."

Randal halted, one foot on the bottom step. "If it's about those rats I charmed out of your pantry, I told you a long-term warding spell costs more than just my room and board."

"No," said the innkeeper. "Day by day is fine. They're still gone. But if you could do the same for the fleas and the bedbugs . . ."

"Ten coppers," Randal said automatically.

"Six," the innkeeper replied.

"Eight," said Randal. "Half in advance."

"Done," said the innkeeper. "I'll pay you in the morning."

Randal smiled to himself as he mounted the steep steps to the upstairs hall. *Eight copper pennies, and five more in my pocket—not bad.* Compared to the riches he'd left behind when he chose to study wizardry instead of becoming a knight, thirteen pennies didn't look like much—but here in Cingestoun, one penny was more than enough to buy a meal at the Green Bough, and sleeping space on the floor besides.

His own small use of magic had done him even better, purchasing the luxury of a room upstairs. As he paused with one hand on the latch, he murmured the words of the doorkeeping spell. An alarm sounded in his mind. Someone had entered his room since the morning, and that someone was still there.

Nick's words of caution came to him. Was there a thief waiting inside? *Well, he'll be the one getting the surprise,* Randal thought as he prepared a shock spell. Then he opened the door and stepped into the room—only to come to a sudden halt on the other side of the threshold.

Magic! Unfamiliar magic. The scar on his right palm began to throb. But this magic was strange, like nothing he had known before. Randal called up a

12

small ball of cold-flame and looked around the room by its eerie, blue-white glow.

He heard a creaking noise from the bed in the corner. Heart pounding, he spun toward the sound.

"Wizard . . ."

The faint whisper came from his bed. Randal looked and saw a man lying there, his features drawn and ashen in the cold blue light. Randal forced himself to go over to the cot and grasp the man by the shoulder.

One touch and the young wizard pulled his hand back. The man lying on the bed wore the ragged traces of what once had been a journeyman's robe like Randal's own, now grown soiled and tattered with age. But it wasn't the torn robe that had caused Randal to draw away; it was the sickening, hollow feeling he experienced when his fingers closed on the man's shoulder—as if the man was both empty and filled with a sense of power and energy greater than Randal had ever before encountered.

*He's dying,* Randal thought. *Dying of magic.*

Randal prepared the most powerful healing spell he knew, one that he'd learned earlier in the summer from master wizard Balpesh. He fought back a shudder of revulsion at the thought of touching that dead-but-living flesh a second time and laid his hand on the man's cold, sweating forehead. In a low voice, he murmured the spell of restoration, and he felt his own magical energies flowing out into the dying man, helping his weakened lungs to take in air and his laboring heart to beat.

"*Spira.*" He whispered the spell words again in the Old Tongue, the language that all wizards used to cast their spells and record their magical observations. "*Spira vive-que.*"

But Randal knew in his heart that the magic wasn't strong enough. Whatever was killing the stranger kept on drawing strength—the more Randal gave to the spell, the more it took from the man he was trying to heal. At last, the young wizard pulled away, defeated.

The attempt had given the man some strength, at least. He raised himself up from the thin mattress and said again, "Wizard. They told me you were a wizard, down below. You have to help me."

"I am trying to help you," said Randal as calmly as he could. *What good is knowing how to stop bleeding and lower a fever, against something like this?* he wondered. *How do you cure a man under a death spell? Balpesh would know.*

But Balpesh was a master wizard who'd spent years learning the healer's art, and Randal was only a journeyman. Already, the effects of Randal's spell were starting to fade. With the last of his strength, the stranger brought something out from under the pillow where it had lain hidden: a leather bag closed with a drawstring cord.

"Take this," he said. "Help me."

Randal hesitated. Something about the sack—the way it seemed to press down the man's hand with an unnatural weight, or the way shadows collected in its folds—hinted at the presence of powerful magic. *What manner of thing is this?* he wondered. Magical

14

objects were not accepted carelessly, but he felt drawn toward it just the same.

"Please," said the stranger. "You are a wizard . . . you will know what to do. . . ." His breath came in ragged gasps, and he had to pause before going on. "Dagon wants this . . . he waits at the Rooster and Roundels."

Still, Randal paused. The object in the bag seemed to call to him and repulse him at the same time. Before he could act, the stranger collapsed back onto the pillow and the leather bag fell from his lifeless hand.

Randal stood for a moment in shock. He had seen death before, but never like this, in a man he'd been trying to help. And never death caused by magic.

*Worse yet,* Randal thought numbly, *the man made a request, calling on me as a wizard. And as a wizard, I can't refuse.*

He picked up the sack. It was lighter than he had expected it would be from the way the stranger had handled it. A cold feeling walked up his spine.

*There's powerful magic here indeed,* he thought. *But not of any kind that I've ever known before.*

The wisest course of action, Randal knew, would be to hand over the bag unopened to Dagon, whoever he might be—but curiosity, as they said at the Schola, was always a wizard's greatest vice. *And after all, that's why the Schola sends apprentices out to be journeymen—to learn more about magic.*

Carefully, Randal opened the bag and peeled it away from the object it contained: a little statue about a foot tall, carved from ivory long since gone

golden with age, representing an old woman leaning on a staff.

He held up the carving and looked at it from all angles. It was more than well made—the old woman almost seemed real. Each wrinkle of her face was lovingly rendered. The hand that grasped the staff was knobby and thin. A few strands of hair escaped from under her hood. Looking at it, Randal got the odd sensation that the figure was alive.

He shuddered slightly. The feeling of magic was overwhelming. Fortunately, the statue wasn't his problem. It was Dagon's. All that remained was to find this Dagon and get rid of the unsettling piece of artwork.

# II.
# Midnight Dealings

RANDAL SLIPPED THE little statue back into its protective sack. He paused for a moment to examine the leather—soft and fine, like the best pigskin, but even more delicate. Pulling the drawstrings tight, he tied the sack to his belt and then looked down at the dead man lying in his bed. He didn't like the idea of just leaving him there, but the man had died trying to hand over the bag and what it contained.

"Whatever your name was," he promised the dead man, "I'll try to get back soon and take care of you—but I'll carry out your errand first. Wherever you've gone, fare well."

Randal extinguished the cold-flame, stepped out into the hall, and cast a locking spell on the bedroom door. As he finished, he heard a familiar light tread coming up the stairs and turned to see Lys, with her lute in its leather case slung over her shoulder.

She looked at him curiously. "You're going back out at this hour? I thought you were going to turn in early."

"I was," said Randal. "But something . . . came up, and I have to take care of it."

She looked at him sharply. "Trouble?"

"Bad trouble," said Randal. "There's a dead man in my bed, and magic killed him."

Even in the dim light, he could see her eyes widen and her lips move in an exclamation in her native southlands tongue. Then she dropped back into the language of Brecelande again and asked, "*You* didn't—?"

"No," said Randal. "I never have, and I don't even know if I could. I don't know what happened to him. But before he died, he gave me an errand to run."

"And that's where you're headed now?"

Randal nodded. "To a place called the Rooster and Roundels. Do you know how to find it?"

"You're not going there alone?" Lys asked sharply.

"Yes, I am," said Randal. The statue in its leather bag made a heavy weight at his belt. "I've been given something I don't understand," he said, "and I don't want my friends getting in trouble on my account."

"The Rooster and Roundels is over near the river docks," said Lys. "You can't go there alone. You'll need someone to watch your back."

"I can take care of myself," said Randal.

"Right," said Lys. She didn't sound convinced.

Randal sighed. "Since you're probably going to follow me whether I ask you to or not, you might as well come along."

A damp fog had risen outside, making Randal glad of the thick cloth of his wizard's robe as he and

19

Lys made their way to the dockside district. The River Donchess, flowing out of the dense Wilderness of Lannad to the west, ran through the center of Cingestoun, and the boatmen gathered in cheap inns along the waterfront. The street facing the river was lined with rough, dangerous places, of which the Rooster and Roundels looked to be one of the worst: foul smelling and dimly lit by a scattering of smoky rushlights.

"This is the sort of place I wouldn't sing in without an armed guard," Lys muttered as she and Randal stepped through the door and into the hazy common room. She stuck close to his shoulder and kept one hand on the hilt of the small knife she wore at her belt.

Randal nodded agreement. "If I hadn't made a promise to a dead man," he said, "I wouldn't be here."

He'd already marked how the boatmen and gamblers drinking at the rough-hewn tables had eyed them as they entered, and then had looked away again. *Nick worries too much,* he thought. *They still recognize a wizard's robes.* The knowledge gave him a little more confidence. A couple of boys—for so Lys appeared at a casual glance—might be ripe victims for robbery, kidnapping, or worse, but a wizard was something else.

Just the same, Randal scanned the room warily as he and Lys made their way through the close-packed tables to where the landlord stood filling tankards from an open keg. *Two doors . . . windows on three walls . . . lots of ways in and out . . . and as scummy a bunch of wharf rats as I've ever seen.*

"I'm looking for Dagon," Randal said to the landlord. "Is he here tonight?"

"Maybe," said the landlord. He eyed Randal narrowly. "What's it to you, wizard?"

"Private business," said Randal. He reached into the deep inside pocket of his journeyman's robe, past the small leatherbound spell book that he kept there, and pulled out one of the five copper pennies. The young wizard held out the coin. In the orange glow from the rushlights, the long scar across his palm made a raised white line against the surrounding flesh.

"Can you point Dagon out for me?" he asked.

The landlord took the coin. "Over there," he said, nodding toward a table where a dark, thickset man sat with his back to the wall. "That's him."

Randal frowned briefly as he took in the dark man's studded jacket of hardened leather—the armor of a mercenary foot soldier. *A fighting man? For something like this, I was expecting a wizard. That man in my room had to know more than a little of the Art, or he'd never have gotten past the spells on my door. But this fellow . . .*

Dagon watched without expression as Randal and Lys crossed to his table and took seats facing him. Randal began the conversation without buildup. "Are you Dagon?"

The dark man took a deliberate pull from his mug before answering. "I don't think I know you."

"If you *are* Dagon," Randal continued, "then I met a man today who said he had something for you."

A gleam of interest showed in the stranger's eyes.

"And if I *was* Dagon, then what would that thing be?"

"A statue."

Dagon let out his breath in what could have been either satisfaction or relief. "Bryce got it, then. What does he want for it? Tell him that I already paid him, and he won't get a copper more."

*That's the truth,* thought Randal, *whether you meant it to be or not.*

"It isn't like that," he said. "He asked me to give it to you. . . ."

Dagon sat up straighter and leaned forward. "You have it here? Hand it over."

Seeing the avid gleam in Dagon's eyes, Randal suddenly felt reluctant to pass the ivory carving across. *That statue holds powerful magic of a kind I've never experienced—what could a man like this want with such a thing? He isn't going to think past the money it'll bring him when he sells it.*

Still, giving the statue to Dagon had been the dying man's own request. *Since you couldn't save him,* Randal told himself, *you ought to at least do that.*

He took the bag from his belt and opened it. Reaching in, he pulled out the figurine. "Is this what you were expecting?"

Randal set the carving upright in the center of the table. The flickering light made it seem as if the old woman was in motion, even though she was only dead ivory. Once again, Randal felt the prickling sensation that told of powerful magic.

"Yes," Dagon said. "That's mine." The mercenary reached out to take the carving.

22

Before his hands could close around it, the two doors of the Rooster and Roundels smashed open. A dozen armored men in yellow surcoats came crashing in, their swords out and ready. Randal heard the racket of a table falling over, and the metallic whisper of a broadsword coming out of its sheath. Then the six windows of the tavern's bottom story crashed in, and more men-at-arms came clambering through, swords drawn.

"Fess's men!" exclaimed Dagon, leaping to his feet and drawing his sword as he rose. "Time to get out of here."

The table rocked and tilted dangerously when he bumped into it, and the ivory figurine started sliding toward the floor. Lys grabbed the statue as the table went over, and she thrust the carved figure out toward Randal. His fingers wrapped around the cold ivory.

"Give it to him and let's run," she said hurriedly. "It's not our quarrel." Then her eyes widened and she cried out, "Quick, Randy—duck!"

He ducked, and a sword-blade whizzed over his head as one of the yellowcoated men took a swing at him. The young wizard flashed a bright light in the man's face and boomed some thunder in his ear— easy spells, but enough to stun the man and buy some thinking time.

"We're with you," Randal said to Dagon. "Let's go."

The three went out the nearest window. The street outside held more men, wearing the same yellow surcoats as those in the tavern. Some of them carried torches, and all of them were armed. Randal

23

called up another flash of light into the midst of the troop, this time making it bright enough to dazzle the yellowcoats into temporary blindness.

"This way!" yelled Dagon. "Hurry!"

The mercenary led the pair down a winding alley. Randal and Lys followed, running lightly, their leather soles making only a faint slapping sound against the fog-slicked cobblestones.

A few minutes later, the three paused in the shadow of some empty casks stacked at the foot of one of the city wharves.

"That wasn't bad, what you did back there," said Dagon. "A wizard, are you?"

"You saw for yourself," Randal told him. *No point in letting him know I'm only a journeyman. A wizard doesn't lie . . . but what a man thinks is his own business.* "And I don't like what's going on. Who's Fess, and why is he after you?"

Dagon chuckled grimly. "You must be new around here if you don't know who Lord Fess is. And he's not just after me anymore—not since everybody in the Rooster and Roundels saw you handing over that piece of ivory. Speaking of which . . ."

Randal shook his head. "Not until you tell me what it is and why you want it. For something that small, it's caused too much trouble already."

"I don't know what it is," Dagon admitted. "All I know is that Varnart wants it, and he's paying good money for it. That's enough for me."

"Not for us," said Lys, at the same time as Randal asked, "Who's Varnart?"

"I thought all you wizards knew each other," said

Dagon. "The statue is really his—or so he told me. He only wanted it back."

"Sure he did," said Lys. "Tell us another."

Randal ignored her. "If the statue is Varnart's, then who is Fess?"

Dagon gave a world-weary sigh. "Cingestoun's a free town, but Lord Fess holds just about everything outside the city walls. And sometimes things turn up in his treasure room that don't have any business being there, if you take my drift."

Lys put her hands on her hips and looked straight at the mercenary. "You stole it, didn't you?"

"Not me," said Dagon. "That was Bryce's job. I'm just returning the carving to its rightful owner."

Randal's lips tightened, and he folded his arms on his chest. "So you took the safe part for yourself."

"You call being chased halfway across Cingestoun by Fess's yellowcoats 'safe'?" said Dagon indignantly.

Randal nodded. "Bryce is already dead."

"I see," said Dagon. "Too bad. He was a friend of mine." He gave the young wizard a measuring glance. "Your doing?"

There was a note in the mercenary's voice that Randal didn't like at all. *I don't want to fight this man,* he thought. *I'd have to use something a lot more permanent than bright lights and loud noises.*

"I found him in my room," Randal said aloud. Carefully, in the back of his mind, he began readying a shock spell in case he needed it. "I don't know how he got there, but he was already dying. He gave me the statue and said it was for you."

"If that's what happened," Lys cut in, "then I

say let's hand the thing over and say good night."

"It's not that simple," Randal replied. "Not with magic involved." In fact, he felt less and less sure that he ought to give the statue to Dagon. The mercenary clearly had no idea how to deal with a magical artifact. True, Randal had promised . . . but only to find Dagon, nothing more.

*Maybe I ought to give the statue to Varnart myself,* he thought. *Wizard to wizard. If we're dealing with an artifact of power, that would be the safest thing to do.*

"Let's talk about this someplace warm and dry," Randal said finally. "I think we've shaken Fess's men, so it's probably safe to go back to the Green Bough."

Dagon scowled at him for a moment longer and then shrugged. "Sounds good to me."

But when they reached the Green Bough, Randal stopped short with an exclamation of dismay and gestured the others back into the shadows of the alley. Two men-at-arms in yellow surcoats were coming out of the inn. They took places on either side of the doorstep, as if standing guard.

"I don't like the looks of this," said Lys. "I'm sure nobody back at that other place knew me or Randal by sight, so how could they have gotten here before we did?"

"Bryce," said Dagon. "Someone must have followed him into town." The mercenary shook his head. "Careless of him."

"He was probably dying already," said Randal. "And as soon as somebody breaks down the locking spell on my door, Fess's men are going to find his body."

"Then we'd better leave town," said Lys at once. "You'll never convince Lord Fess that you didn't do it."

"Smart girl," Dagon remarked—apparently Lys's disguise hadn't survived the conversation. "I have to meet a fellow outside town tomorrow anyway. But getting out of Cingestoun's likely to be harder than it sounds. Fess's men will be watching all the gates by now, and those fellows who hit the Rooster and Roundels got a good look at all of us."

Lys bit her lip. "So what do we do now, Randy? Climb over the walls?"

"I've heard worse ideas," said Dagon. "But we'd still have to reckon with city guards."

Lys wasn't paying any attention to the mercenary. "Well?" she asked, still looking at Randal.

"Let me think. . . ." The young wizard frowned. *I've never been all that good with disguises and illusions,* he thought. *I couldn't cover all three of us, or even just Lys and me, for more than a little while. Not if we're all moving. And fighting our way out's no good either—not when we're one mercenary, a lute-player, and a journey-man wizard up against Lord Fess's personal troops. We'll have to smuggle ourselves through the gates somehow. . . .*

"I've got it," he said. "Come on."

Dagon didn't move. "Where are you going?"

"I have a friend in town," said Randal. "With any kind of luck, Fess's men don't know about him, and with a bit more luck, he'll be willing to help us."

The young wizard led the way back along the route he had followed at the start of the evening, from the Green Bough to Carpenters' Lane. Now the sky overhead was beginning to go from black to gray, and the stars were gone. Soon a smell of resin and sawdust filled the dawn air.

"Nick's shop is close by here," said Randal to Lys. A moment later he stopped before a barred and shuttered shopfront.

Dagon frowned. "How do we get in without waking up the whole street?" the mercenary asked.

"Like this," Randal said, laying his hand on the shop door. He muttered a quiet spell of opening, and the bolt shifted. He pushed at the door, and it swung open. "Let's get inside before somebody spots us."

Once all three of them were inside the shop, Randal called up a sphere of cold-flame. The blue light played over the workbench and the tools, the carpenters' aprons hanging from pegs along the walls, the motes of sawdust, and a curled wood-shaving that had escaped the evening cleanup. Dagon looked about the shop with a fighter's usual contempt for a tradesman, but Lys's dark blue eyes were interested and a little sad.

"This is a long way from the Schola," she murmured.

"It's honest work," said Randal, in the same low tones. "And safer than life on the road. You two stay down here, and I'll go wake up Nick."

He started for the stairs that led to the upper levels of the shop but stopped at a muffled exclamation from Dagon.

"Someone's coming!" said the mercenary.

Randal turned and saw that Dagon already had

his sword half-drawn. "Put that away," said Randal. "I told you, this man's a friend."

Dagon looked unconvinced. "Yours maybe—not mine." The mercenary met Randal's gaze for a long minute before slamming the sword back into its scabbard.

By the time he had done so, Nick was already coming down the stairs into the blue glow of the cold-flame, a heavy wooden club at the ready in his right hand.

# III.

# A Friend in Need

"WHAT," SAID RANDAL, half laughing, "a club and not a dagger?"

"Old habits die hard," said Nick, tucking the club into his belt with a look of relief. "I suppose I stayed too long at Tarnsberg. I still don't feel right about using steel." He saw Lys and broke into a delighted smile. "Lys! I've been looking forward to seeing you ever since Randy told me you were in town. But what brings you to the shop at this hour?"

"We have to get past the town gates without being spotted," Randal answered. "Can you help us?"

"Are you in trouble?"

"Not if we aren't seen," Lys replied.

"Then there's nothing easier," said Nick. "Mind telling me who's chasing you, just so I'll know who to avoid?"

"Fess's men," said Randal. "We have something they want, and they're acting serious about getting it."

Nick frowned. "Those yellowcoats are a nasty bunch. I'll still help you, but I'd like to know what you're trying to keep away from them."

"This," said Randal. He unwrapped the ivory statue from the bag that protected it and set it down on the carpenter's workbench. As before, the old woman seemed to have moved since the last time he'd seen her, even though he couldn't pinpoint a particular change. "I think it's an artifact of power."

Nick reached out to touch the smooth ivory of the carving. He ran a forefinger along the curve of the figure's wrinkled cheek and then drew his hand back with an odd expression. "It's . . . certainly something very strange," he said. "I don't recall ever reading or hearing about anything like it."

"Me, neither," said Randal. "So what do you think?"

Nick stroked his curly brown beard, all the while frowning at the ivory figurine. "I haven't done magic since I quit the Schola," he said finally, "and that thing still makes my skin prickle. I'd say get rid of it as soon as you can—but not to Lord Fess."

"Don't worry," said Dagon. "I've already got a buyer."

Nick glanced over at the mercenary, and then back to Randal. When he spoke again, it was in the Old Tongue. "*Who is that person?*"

"*One of my other problems,*" said Randal, in the same language. "*His name is Dagon, and I don't trust him. He says the artifact is supposed to go to someone called Varnart.*"

"*I see,*" said Nick. He switched back to the language of Brecelande. "Come help me harness up the lumber wagon. The guards at the North Gate are used to passing me through early in the

31

morning when I go to the Oseney woodlots for timber. You can hide in the back of the wagon, and I'll drive you out of town."

A few minutes later, Alured Carpenter's lumber wagon rolled out of the stable in the back of the shop. On the wagon-driver's seat, Nick whistled a cheerful tune as the wagon rumbled down the alley into the broader stretch of Carpenters' Lane. In the box of the wagon, Randal, Lys, and Dagon huddled under a canvas cloth.

*Good thing Nick was in town and willing to help,* Randal thought, as he breathed the close, resin-scented air. *Otherwise I'd be stuck with trying to make the three of us look like rag collectors or something.*

"Your friend could get a pretty sum from Fess for turning us in," Dagon muttered low-voiced at Randal's elbow.

"Don't worry," said Lys. Even in the darkness, Randal could tell that she was angry. "Nick wouldn't even think of doing a thing like that."

"You'd better hope he doesn't try," said Dagon. "If I so much as get suspicious—"

"You'll keep your mouth shut and hold still," Randal said sharply. "I told you before, Nick is my friend."

The whistling from the driver's seat stopped. "Better be quiet back there," Nick whispered. "We're coming up on the North Gate."

Randal half knelt and peered through a chink in the wooden slats that formed the front and sides of the lumber wagon. Through the narrow gap, he could see Nick's head and shoulders silhouetted against the orange torchlight coming from the North Gate guardhouse. Armed men moved about in the road ahead.

*Yellow surcoats,* observed Randal, as the lumber wagon trundled closer to the guardhouse. *Dagon was right. Fess's men are watching the gates already.* He turned and whispered to the others, "Don't move. I may have to try an illusion to get us past."

Nick drove the lumber wagon up to the guardhouse and then brought the four-horse team to a halt. Randal watched from beneath the canvas as the regular night guard came up, holding a lantern. A pair of yellowcoated men came with the gatekeeper, one on either side.

Randal pursed his lips in a silent whistle and shook his head. *Lord Fess isn't taking any chances.*

"Where do you think you're going?" one of the yellowcoats demanded.

"Out to Oseney," Nick called back. "Ebert, tell these fellows who I am."

The night guard held up the lantern so that the yellow light shone directly on Nick's face. Randal, crouched in the wagon-box and squinting through the little space between the canvas and the wood, saw that his friend's lips were tight and his jaw was set under the dense brown beard.

The guard gave Nick no more than a cursory glance before lowering his lantern with a nod. "I know you," he said. He turned to the yellowcoat on his right. "It's just Alured Carpenter's journeyman. He comes by here three, four times every month."

Fess's man frowned. He took a step forward and

looked up at Nick. "You, journeyman—what brings you through the gates this early in the morning?"

Randal tensed. He heard the catch in Lys's breathing and the faint sliding sound of her dagger coming out of its sheath. From Dagon he heard nothing at all—and that, he somehow knew, was an even more dangerous sign. *It's not enough that I have to worry about the gate guards,* thought Randal. *If Dagon gets it into his head that Nick's sold us out . . .*

But Nick only ran a hand across his face as if he were still half-asleep and blinked down at the guard. "I need wood, the same as always, and it's a long way out to Oseney."

The regular guard scratched his head. "Didn't you come through looking for wood just three days past?"

Nick swallowed a yawn and then shrugged. "Business is good lately. I go fetch wood when Alured tells me to."

The second of Fess's men nodded at the four-horse team. "Why so many horses to pull the wagon?"

Nick yawned again. "Load's heavy sometimes."

"Then you won't mind if I look in the back."

The words were a statement, not a question, and the yellowcoat had already headed around toward the rear of the wagon before Nick could reply. Randal clenched his hands on the rim of the wagon-box and pressed his forehead against the wood.

*Illusion,* he thought, listening to the heavy footsteps growing closer. We need an *illusion.*

He closed his eyes and spoke the words that

34

created a false appearance. As he finished, the guard's footsteps reached the back of the wagon. He couldn't hear Lys's breathing at all now, and the silence from Dagon seemed even heavier than before. If the mercenary decided to make good on his earlier threat, there was no way Randal could stop him—not without dropping the fragile illusion spell first.

Randal heard the stiff rustle of the canvas being lifted and felt cold sweat break out on his forehead with the effort of keeping up the illusion.

*Bare boards and shadows . . . let Fess's man see only bare boards and shadows.*

The canvas rustled again as the guard let it drop. The footsteps went back around to the front of the wagon, and Randal heard the voices of the three guards in muttered conference.

"She's empty, all right. You vouch for this man, Ebert?"

"Known him this past year or more, and a more honest sort you won't find between here and Widsegard."

"Right, then. Off you go, carpenter . . . and if you happen to see a pair of boys and a man-at-arms anywhere between here and Oseney, make certain you tell us about it double quick."

Randal heard Nick give another smothered yawn as the gates creaked open. "I'll keep an eye out," promised the apprentice wizard turned carpenter, and then he called to the horses: "Gee up!"

The lumber wagon lurched forward and rolled out through the North Gate into the graying light of dawn. With a sigh of relief, Randal let the illusion go. He was shivering as he sank back down to a seated position on the wagon-bed, and his teeth were chattering.

He felt the light touch of Lys's hand on his arm. "Are you all right, Randy?"

The young wizard nodded, although he knew she couldn't see him in the darkness under the canvas. "I'm fine—just tired, that's all. Illusions are hard work."

*Especially when you've never been very good at them in the first place,* he added to himself, but he knew better than to say it out loud. Only Dagon's grudging respect for his magical skills had kept the mercenary cooperative so far. *If he ever figures out how little I really know, he'll kill me the next time I turn my back.*

"Rest while you can," came Nick's voice from the front of the wagon. "I'm taking the three of you well clear of town before I stop the wagon and let you off."

"Do what Nick says," Lys told Randal. "I'll keep alert in case of trouble."

Randal started to protest and found himself yawning instead. Almost in spite of himself, he leaned back against the side of the wagon and fell asleep.

He woke to the feel of the wagon coming to a halt. A moment later, pale light struck his closed eyelids, and he opened his eyes to see Nick pulling back the canvas cover from the wagon-box. Randal looked around and saw nothing, for the moment, that appeared threatening or even interesting—only the nondescript brown and green of the grasslands that surrounded Cingestoun. The sky overhead was gray and watery, and a light mist dampened everything as soon as the canvas was raised.

"We're almost to Oseney," said Nick. The journey-man carpenter was smiling cheerfully, in spite of the beads of moisture silvering his brown hair and beard. "That was a good job you did back there at the gate. I was afraid we were done for."

Lys pushed herself away from the side of the wagon and stretched. Her lute, which she'd carried with her during all the night's adventures, lay on the floor of the wagon near her feet. "So was I," she said to Nick. "Thanks, Randy."

Randal shrugged. "The dark night, the torchlight, the fact that they didn't really expect to find us . . . it wasn't all that much work, as illusions go."

Next to Randal, Dagon sat up and yawned. The mercenary had fallen asleep himself on the road out of Cingestoun; wood chips and scraps of bark from the floor of the wagon clung to his hair and clothing. "It was enough," he said as he brushed himself off. "Now that we're past the gates, you can hand over Bryce's package like you agreed."

Randal shook his head. "Oh, no. I never agreed to that." He closed his hand around the statue inside its leather bag. "We were going to talk things over at the Green Bough."

Dagon turned to face Randal directly. "You're quibbling, wizard. That statue doesn't belong to you. It's Varnart's, and I'm going to see that it goes to him." He looked at Randal for a moment. "I thank

37

you for your help so far, and now I'll thank you to hand over that carving."

"I know it's not mine," said Randal. "I don't want it, and I'll be happy to get rid of it. But I'm going to give it to Varnart myself."

Lys gave him a doubtful glance. "Are you sure you want to get yourself mixed up in something like this?"

"No," Randal said. "But there's something about that statue . . . take a good look at it."

He opened the leather bag and pulled out the ivory figurine. The light of day brought out even more clearly the fineness of the unknown artist's work: He could see the very wrinkles on the knuckles of the old woman's hand where it gripped the staff, and her eyes, under their deep brows, seemed ready to blink and gaze about.

Lys regarded the figurine for a long moment. "If that thing were mine," she said finally, "I'd drop it in a well. I don't like the looks of it."

Surprisingly, Dagon nodded. "I don't either, but Varnart's the one who's paying for it. And don't think you'll be getting a reward for giving him that piece," he added suspiciously. "His agreement was with me and me alone."

"You can have Varnart's money," said Randal. "I don't want that either. But I'm almost certain this statue is an artifact of power. If that's so, then you need a wizard to handle it."

"I had Bryce," said Dagon. "But you tell me he's dead."

Nick was frowning. "If Randy says your friend's

dead," he told the mercenary, "then he's dead. And if that thing really is an artifact of power, then the sooner it gets safely to Varnart and out of our hands, the better."

"For a carpenter, you sure talk a lot about magic," Dagon said. He looked at Nick curiously. "What' s an artifact of power?"

Randal slid the ivory carving back into its protective bag. "All objects contain magic," he explained. For a moment, as he considered the mercenary's question, he was back at the Schola in Tarnsberg, sitting safe in a warm, dry room and listening to Master Crannach lecturing on magical theory.

He put the memory behind him and continued. "Most of the time, though, objects don't contain very *much* magic. But once in a while, an object turns up that has so much magic it can act by itself. If it's properly controlled, it can be the key to great things."

Lys looked nervously at the now-closed leather bag. "What happens if it isn't controlled?"

Randal and Nick exchanged glances.

"Then you've got trouble," said Nick. "A thing like that doesn't have much use for people."

Dagon scratched the stubble on his jaw and scowled. "Sounds like a demon to me."

"It's worse. Demons aren't of this world," said Randal, quoting what he had heard during those classes in Tarnsberg that now seemed so long ago. "You can send them back where they came from. But artifacts *are* of this world. They're in this world and contain part of the world in themselves. You can't destroy one without destroying part of your own world, and the world fights that."

"And you think Varnart's figurine is one of those artifacts," said Dagon thoughtfully.

Randal nodded. "I'm almost certain of it."

"Then it can't hurt to have a wizard along until I turn it over," said the mercenary at last. "The meeting place isn't too far from here. We can make it on foot if we have to."

"No need," said Nick. "You three wait here, and I'll take the lumber wagon to Oseney and bring the horses back. They know me at the woodlot; Alured's wagon will be safe there while we're on the road."

"Wait a minute," said Randal. " 'We'?"

"I'm coming with you," said the one-time apprentice wizard. He grinned through his beard at Randal. "This one looks like too much fun to miss."

"It's your neck," grunted Dagon as he climbed out of the wagon. The mercenary looked back at Randal and Lys. "Come on. The less time we spend hanging around by the side of the road, the better."

Lys vaulted over the side of the wagon with an acrobat's easy grace. Randal followed more slowly and stood for a moment leaning against his walking staff. Nick called to the horses, and the wagon creaked off down the road.

# IV.
## Power

"LET'S GO," said Dagon. "That wooded patch over there looks good enough for laying up awhile."

Soon Randal, Lys, and Dagon were sitting on their cloaks in the middle of a stand of trees. This close to the great Wilderness of Lannad, the ancient forest that extended across southern Brecelande, the trees were dense and old. The light mist of early morning had thickened into a steady drizzle. The drops of water collected on the twigs and branches overhead and plopped heavily down onto the dead leaves below.

"So far, so good," said Dagon. "I'm close to the place where I'm supposed to meet Varnart, and in plenty of time. Just as long as Fess's yellowcoats aren't coming along behind. . . ." He looked at Randal. "You're a wizard—can you tell if anybody is chasing us?"

Randal stifled a groan. *Please,* he thought, *not when I'm already hurting all over.* His joints and muscles ached from the bumpy ride in the lumber wagon, and his head felt fuzzy from lack of sleep. But with Dagon watching he didn't dare refuse.

"Give me something I can look into," he told the mercenary. "A dish of clear water's best, or a crystal, but we haven't got either of those. Ordinary polished metal will work in a pinch."

"Crystal, did you say?" Dagon pulled his dagger from its sheath on his belt and held out the weapon hilt first. It was a fighter's weapon, long-bladed and double-edged, with a metal cross guard—forged for use, not for beauty. The massive blue gemstone set into the pommel looked out of place against the plain metal.

"Yes," said Randal. "That will work."

The mercenary regarded the sapphire with a fond expression. "I've had good luck with it myself," he said. "I've pawned it a dozen times if I've pawned it once, and I've always been able to buy it back."

Randal took the dagger. His scarred hand closed awkwardly on the grip, reminding him again that he had forsworn the use of such weapons when he first set out to study the wizard's art. He'd broken that vow only once, to stop his teacher, Master Laerg, from destroying the entire School of Wizardry—and he'd almost lost his own magic as a result.

*This is different,* he told himself. *You're using the stone, not the steel.*

He planted the dagger point first in the earth—ignoring Dagon's squawk of protest—and focused his attention on the sapphire. Time passed. He could sense Dagon and Lys moving about restlessly, somewhere outside his narrowed range of vision. He forced away the awareness of them, willing himself to sink deeper and deeper into the sapphire's azure depths.

A light flickered within the gem. It steadied and showed a nest in a tree—a bird's nest, but empty and broken, with a small bird perched forlornly on a nearby twig. Beneath the tree, a yellow-eyed cat circled. The bird took fright and flew off. The cat grew yellow feathers and became a bird of prey, a golden falcon that mounted skyward and followed as the bird flew on.

As Randal bent down to see the images better, a harsh oath broke his concentration, and a hand swept down and pulled the dagger free of the earth.

"Your friend's back," said Dagon. "Haven't you seen anything yet?"

Randal's head ached. He pressed his palms against his forehead. *Yellow eyes . . . yellow feathers . . . yellow, like the surcoats.*

"Fess's men," he muttered. "Following behind us."

"Close?" That was Nick's voice.

"Not yet, I think." Randal used his walking staff to pull himself to his feet. He turned to Dagon. "Let's get on to your meeting. The sooner we can hand over that carving to Varnart, the safer we'll all be."

The mercenary wiped the dirt off his dagger and slammed it back into its sheath. "Right. Everybody mount up. We're making for a ruined watchtower about a league past the turn-off for Oseney. The meeting with Varnart is supposed to take place halfway between noon and sunset. Let's go."

They rode for a couple of hours and reached the watchtower at about midafternoon, just as the rain was ending and the clouds were breaking up. Once, the tower had stood to keep the High King's peace, but now its moss-grown walls were open to the sky, and the fallen roof lay in rubble on the floor.

Randal glanced about at the piles of stones half covered with dead leaves and dirt. "You're sure this is the place?"

"Of course I'm sure," said Dagon. He turned to Lys and Nick. "You two stay outside and hold the horses. This'll just be the wizard and me."

Nick ignored the mercenary. "Do you want me along, Randy?"

The journeyman wizard shook his head. "Don't worry—I can handle it. As soon as Varnart shows up, I'll give him the carving and that'll be that."

Dagon and Randal walked through an empty doorway into the shell of the watchtower. Lys and Nick stayed outside, out of sight behind the curving wall.

Inside the tower, Randal and Dagon waited while the afternoon shadows grew slowly longer. Randal sat on a block of stone and watched the sunlight shift across the wall. Dagon paced about restlessly, moving from door to window to broken wall, one hand always on the hilt of his sword.

Then a lean man—tall, dressed in elegant gray clothing, clean-shaven that very morning—stepped without warning through a gap in the crumbling stone. Randal came to his feet at once, but the stranger seemed not to notice him. Instead, he looked at Dagon and smiled.

"It's always a pleasure," the man said, "to deal with someone who keeps his word. Did you have any trouble getting the object?"

Dagon halted his pacing and faced the new arrival. "Just who are you, anyway?" he asked. His feet were planted wide, and his right hand gripped his sword hilt. "Too many people I don't know are mixed up in this already."

"I come from the one who hired you," said the newcomer. "I have orders to pay you, but I warn you, sir, I have also been instructed that I must not return without the carving." He gave a slight nod to one side, and two other men stepped out of hiding from behind the stones. These men were also dressed in gray and carried swords and daggers.

Dagon looked from one of the armed men to the other, without moving a hairsbreadth from where he stood. "If you've got the gold, I've got the statue. But first, tell me the name of the man who hired you."

While the two mercenaries spoke, Randal was at work casting a spell of magical resonance: a simple spell, but one that would, if done correctly, tell him whether another wizard was nearby. As he'd half expected, the only magical echo for miles around came from the carving itself. The stranger who stood before them was no wizard . . . as if the sword at his hip had not already proved that to be true.

The tall man laughed a bit, but his smile did not reach his eyes. They were cold gray in the afternoon sunlight. "I am hired by Master Varnart, to fetch back a statue of a woman, so big . . ." The man held up his hands a little less than a foot apart. "So, as one hireling to another, take your payment and be gone."

Dagon turned to Randal. "Give it to him."

Randal hesitated. This man was a stranger and no wizard. But he came from Varnart, whose claim to the statue was as good as anybody's. Randal held out the leather bag.

The tall man pulled the bag into his hands. He opened it, lifted out the statue, examined it briefly, and put it back into the sack. He nodded again and stepped back.

A whisper of sound in the grass outside made Randal turn his head. Lys and Nick came around the broken wall into the tower, walking at sword-point before three more of the gray-clad men.

The stranger smiled. "Good," he said. "Now kill them."

"Double-crosser!" Dagon yelled, drawing his sword and sidestepping at the same time, so that a sudden lunge by one of the men in gray passed cleanly by him.

In the same brief instant between the tall man's order and his men's response, Lys somersaulted forward like the acrobat she was. She curled into a tight ball as she rolled away through the debris. The sword thrust aimed at her shoulderblades passed over her as she spun.

Randal stepped back as well and cast a shock spell at the leader of the band. But the hastily prepared magical blow did nothing, its power fading even before it reached its target. Too late, Randal saw the bronze medallion on the stranger's chest.

*It's an amulet,* Randal realized. *He's protected against magic.*

Randal tried another shock spell, this time at one

of the two men who were attacking Dagon. The man he aimed at staggered and missed his stroke. Dagon took advantage of the distraction to cripple the man with a leg blow before turning back to his one remaining foe.

Randal glanced around again. Lys was nowhere to be seen, but Nick had taken a wound, and now the former apprentice was retreating step by step in front of two men who paced toward him, trying to get him into killing range. Soon his back would be to the wall.

Then Randal lost track of the others as he, too, was attacked by a sword-wielding fighter with murder in mind. *I don't want to use lightning,* he thought, blocking the first blow with his walking staff. *It might kill him, and this isn't really my quarrel.*

Instead, he cast a heat spell on the hilt of the man's sword. Flesh sizzled, and the man dropped his weapon. *I can't use steel,* Randal thought, *but I'm not helpless.*

He swung his walking staff against the man's skull, and the attacker went down. In the momentary breathing space, he looked around and saw that Nick's assailants had backed the journeyman carpenter up against the wall on the other side of the rubble. The two men were about to strike when a heavy chunk of rock crashed down onto the head of one. Lys followed it, leaping from the top of the wall to land on the other man's shoulders. Swordsman and player went down together in a tangle of arms and legs.

The leader of the gray men still had not drawn

his sword. *Maybe that's not a sword at all,* Randal thought in alarm. *Just a hilt attached to a sheath, to fool us. Could this man be a wizard himself—his true nature hidden by whatever's protecting him?*

Then Randal saw that the tall stranger was moving—grasping the amulet on his chest, pulling it off and casting it away from him.

*He* is *a wizard,* thought Randal, with sudden conviction. *The same amulet that hid him stopped him from using magic. And now he's going to kill us all if I can't stop him.*

He tried to call up a lightning bolt—but nothing happened. He staggered, exhausted, and barely recovered his balance in time to see the tall wizard's hand move in the opening gestures of a shock spell. Sluggishly, Randal countered with a shielding of his own—and again the spell was weak. Most of the stranger's power came through anyway and sent Randal stumbling backward.

The stranger raised his hand to cast the shock spell again. This time, Randal knew, the blow would be a fatal one.

Then, suddenly, he became aware of another source of power: magical energy stronger and more plentiful than any he had ever felt before. With the last of his failing strength, he dipped into the new source and cast the lightning spell again.

The power tore its way through Randal like a searing flame. For an agonizing moment, the spell threatened to go out of control and turn on him. With a wrench of effort, he mastered it. In the next second a harsh voice he barely recognized as his own cried out in Old Tongue, "*Ruat fulmen!*" and the lightning struck.

The other wizard fell. In the sudden quiet, Randal strode over to where he lay and pulled the bag from his lifeless fingers. Then the rush of power left Randal as suddenly as it had come, and the journeyman wizard collapsed onto the ground, sitting with his head bowed.

*I told Lys just last night that I didn't know if I could kill a man with magic,* he thought unhappily. *And now I have.* He pressed his forehead against his knees and sat there, shivering uncontrollably even though the late-afternoon air was warm.

Before long he heard footsteps and lifted his head to see Lys, Nick, and Dagon coming toward him. Lys was breathing hard, and both men were bleeding. All three sat down near Randal among the dirt and rubble, and for a little while there was silence.

Finally Dagon spoke. "We won," he said.

"So what do we do now?" asked Nick.

"Just savor the fact that you're alive," said Dagon. "The simple pleasures of life are the best."

The mercenary stood up and walked over to the man who had taken the statue. He turned over the body with the toe of his boot and then bent to scoop up the amulet from where it lay on the dirt. "I hope you got good value for your money," he said to the dead man. "As for me, I'll take this pretty toy for my trouble."

Randal shook his head. There was a sour taste in his mouth, and his limbs were trembling from the backlash of the lightning bolt. "Why would Varnart's man want to kill us?" he asked.

"Dead men don't talk," answered Dagon. "It seems that Master Varnart doesn't want me spreading his dirty little secret." The mercenary laughed briefly. "I wonder what sort of reception that fellow would have gotten when he brought the statue home."

"It doesn't matter," said Randal. "Fess's men are still looking for the carving. And we still have it."

His voice sounded hoarse and cracked even now that he'd rested a little. Lys gave him a sudden concerned glance.

"Are you hurt, Randy?"

"No. They didn't touch me."

Nick frowned at him. "I took a sword cut, and I feel better than you look right now. What happened?"

Randal paused for a moment. "I tapped into a source of power," he said finally, "and it was polluted." His mouth tasted of bile. He swallowed and went on, "When a man is dying of thirst, he'll drink from a puddle in the middle of the street, even though the memory of it will turn his stomach for the rest of his life. I just did something like that."

"I hope you're able to ride," said Dagon harshly. "If Fess's men are hunting for that statue, then we need to be somewhere else."

Randal straightened. "I can ride," he said. "But what about you and Nick?"

The mercenary gave a shrug that ended in a grimace. "Neither one of us is going to die before nightfall."

"We'll travel faster if you aren't losing blood the whole time," said Randal. "Give me another moment to rest, and I'll try healing you both."

The spells that stopped bleeding and closed wounds were simple enough that every village heal-wife knew them—so simple that more than one Schola-trained wizard regarded them with scorn. Nevertheless, Randal found that tending Dagon's and Nick's injuries left him drained and exhausted. He could barely haul himself onto the back of one of the draft horses that had pulled Alured Carpenter's lumber wagon.

"All right," said Dagon to Nick when all four had mounted. "Let's go to Oseney and get you started back to Cingestoun with the wagon."

"Sounds good to me," said the carpenter. "With luck, I'll come out of this with nothing more than a few hard words from Alured for taking off without his leave."

"You've already given us help beyond the claims of friendship," Randal said. "I wish I could have stayed in town a little while longer."

They traveled the rest of the way to the road in silence. When they reached the road, Randal saw that the dirt bore traces of the passing of many horses since they'd turned off the track and headed for the tower. He wasn't the only one to notice; Dagon frowned at the sight, and the mercenary's frown grew deeper the closer the four of them got to Oseney.

At length, he turned the frown on Randal. "When you did your scrying, wizard, why didn't you see what just happened?"

"You asked for news of pursuit behind us," said Randal. "So that's what I was looking for. Scrying is like that—you get answers to the questions you ask and not to the ones that you should have asked instead."

"What exactly *did* you see?" asked Nick.

"A yellow cat," said Randal. "And a bird being chased by a golden falcon."

"Fess's men," Nick said with a nod. "Yellow surcoats."

"So I thought," Randal told him. "But you remember how it is—everything has two meanings. At least. It's possible the cat waiting below the nest might have been the ambush—"

"Wait a minute," said Nick. "This cat. Did it come before the falcon or afterward?"

"Before," said Randal. In spite of his exhaustion, he found himself enjoying the discussion. He'd been in dozens like it, back at the Schola, as apprentices and masters pried apart their dreams and visions for the meaning of each detail.

He sat up straighter on the back of Alured's carthorse and went on. "There's more. The bird's nest was broken . . . my room, that Bryce broke into, or Fess's treasury, that Bryce broke into, or Bryce himself, empty of life. Maybe all three at once. And another thing—"

"Birds," said Dagon, in tones of disgust. "Cats. Nests. We're caught between the most powerful wizard and the most powerful warlord for miles around, and you sit there telling animal stories."

"Be careful," Lys cut in sharply. "Someone's coming up the road."

53

# V.

# The Watches of the Night

"IT'S ALL RIGHT," said Nick. "I know that man." He raised his voice and called out, "Ho, now, Swayn Steven's son—any gossip from Oseney?"

The other man—a farmer about Nick's age, carrying a covered basket over one arm—called back, "More than a little, Nick Wariner. I heard you mentioned in the marketplace today."

Dagon glowered. Randal half expected him to attack the unsuspecting Swayn, and the young wizard began readying a shield spell just in case it became necessary to protect the farmer.

But Nick ignored both of them and asked Swayn cheerfully, "Oh? And how did that happen?"

The farmer lowered his voice. "The market was full of men-at-arms in yellow surcoats, asking about anybody who'd come to Oseney from the big town since yesterday—and that's you and no one else. They want to talk to you when you come back from looking at the timber lots. But more than that, they're asking about three strangers."

Swayn pointed with his chin at Randal and the

others. "They're offering silver coin for any word of two boys and a man who look exactly like the ones riding your horses."

"Is that so?" asked Nick.

Swayn nodded. "Not that I've seen anybody like that around here," he added with a wink.

"Thanks for the news," said Nick, smiling in return. "And good day to you."

The farmer touched his cap and said, "Good day to you, too, my friend," to Nick, and walked on past the four riders. Dagon slewed around in his saddle to watch the farmer's departing back and then turned toward Nick and Randal, glaring.

"Cats and birds," he muttered. "What next?"

"I think we'd better forget about the wagon," said Randal.

"These horses still belong to Alured," Nick protested. "I have to get them back to him."

"Today isn't the day to do it," said Lys. "We have to get away. The Wilderness isn't far, but we'll reach it quicker if we keep the horses and ride. From there we can go on foot, and you can go back with the horses. You won't be in any worse trouble, and maybe Fess's men won't be looking for you tomorrow."

"I suppose so," Nick said reluctantly.

"Then enough talking," Dagon snapped. "Let's go."

Darkness overtook them as they traveled, but they continued riding well into the night. Randal kept his seat on the broad back of the carthorse by sheer willpower—aided by the fact that for the first twelve years of his life he had been destined for knight-

55

hood and trained to stay on his horse no matter how hurt he was or how hard the going became.

Finally, he heard Nick say to Dagon, low-voiced, "We have to rest. If we keep this up, we'll kill the horses, and then where will we be?"

"Same place we'll be if Fess's men catch us," replied the mercenary. "Still, stopping's probably worth the risk."

"Randal," Lys asked, "can you hide our camp like you hid us in the wagon?"

Randal shook his head to clear away the fuzziness of exhaustion. "I think so. But not unless it's really necessary—I'd have to stay awake the whole time the illusion is going."

*And even then it'll work only if Fess's men don't trample us by mistake,* he added silently. *And if none of them are looking for magic, and if they haven't guessed exactly how we got out of town this morning. . . .*

"That'll be hard on you," said Nick. "You're as tired as any of us, maybe more."

"I know," said Randal. "But there's no choice. The important thing is to give the horses a chance to rest—you said so yourself."

"And what about you?" asked Lys. Randal couldn't see her face in the dark, but she sounded almost angry. "When do we give *you* a chance to rest?"

"I'll be all right," said Randal. "I can sleep while we're riding if I have to." He gave a tired laugh. "Just pick me up when I fall off."

Lys muttered something in her native Occitanian. A few minutes later, Dagon called a halt. "I hope you're as good as your word, wizard," he told Randal.

56

They settled down for the night. Dagon had found a clearing among some saplings a furlong from where the deeper woods of the Wilderness began. Randal scratched a circle around their camp, drawing a line in the dirt with a pointed stick, but he left the spells themselves uncast. *Time for that,* he thought, *if we come to needing it.*

Then he stretched out on the ground, wrapped himself up in his wizard's robe for warmth, and fell into an exhausted sleep. He woke in the middle of the night to feel Nick shaking him by the shoulder.

"Someone's coming," the carpenter whispered. "You can see them down the slope, using torches to search the ground."

Randal shoved a hand through his hair. "Don't they sleep? Don't their *horses* sleep?"

"Guess not."

"I'll take it from here, then."

Randal cleared his mind, using the techniques he'd learned at the Schola, and spoke the spell of visible illusion. The circle he'd scratched in the dirt earlier flickered for a moment with blue fire, then darkened. Randal sat down on a log near the center and prepared to watch through the night.

"That's it," he said to the others. "You can go back to sleep now."

Dagon looked at him doubtfully. "Is the illusion up?"

Randal shrugged. "Either it is or it isn't."

"You mean you can't tell?"

"Not until somebody sees through it."

Dagon didn't seem happy about that and rolled

57

back up in his cloak with his bare sword close at hand. Within the hour, a troop of yellowcoats appeared, but they passed by the camp without glancing at it. Dagon turned over and began to snore.

Randal relaxed a little. *At least the spell is working,* he thought. After a few minutes, Nick came over and sat beside him. The two looked into the fire in silence for a little while. Then Randal glanced over at Nick. "I've gotten you into a lot of trouble, I'm afraid. Do you have someplace you can go until the search dies down?"

"I'll stick with you," replied the apprentice wizard turned carpenter. "If I'd kept on working at the Art, I'd have been out on the road as a journeyman by now . . . and I've wondered, sometimes, how I would have managed."

"You'd have done fine," said Randal. "Better than I have, certainly." The night air was cold; he pulled his black robe tighter around his shoulders and moved a little closer to the fire. "I never did understand why you left the Schola in the first place. Magic always came so easily to you—a lot easier than it did to me."

"I'm not sure myself why I left," said Nick. For once, his bearded features were serious. "But I couldn't think of any reason why I should stay, either. When it got to where I couldn't recall why I'd left home for the Schola to start with, I knew it was time to quit."

"Home . . ." For a moment, Randal was quiet, fighting the sadness that still came over him some-times when he thought about Castle Doun. *It's been*

58

*more than three years since I left, and who knows if I'll ever see it again. It'll all be changed. . . .*

He glanced over at Nick and saw an expression on the former apprentice's face that mirrored his own feelings. Like most of the students at the Schola, Nick had never spoken much about whatever he might have left behind to study wizardry. *But everybody leaves something,* Randal thought. *And most of us don't go back.*

"Are you from Cingestoun, then?" he asked.

Nick shook his head. "Not me . . . I'm from Widsegard, down on the southern border. I left home bragging that I was going to come back as a wizard or never come back at all."

"So you never went back."

"I couldn't," said Nick. "How could I face the Wizards' Guild in Widsegard, after the way the Guild sent me off to the Schola with such glowing recommendations?"

"Don't let it worry you," Randal said. "Remember what Master Tarn always used to say—'Only one candidate in ten who comes to Tarnsberg is allowed to become an apprentice. And of those, only one in ten goes on to become a journeyman.'"

"I know," Nick replied. "And every night, when I go to bed, I try to convince myself that the reason I didn't become a journeyman was because I wasn't cut out for magic. I keep telling myself that that's the reason—but by the time I'm done, I'm always sure I left because I was afraid to go on. It's no fun waking up every morning thinking I'm a coward."

Nicolas poked at the fire with a stick, knocking the red coals apart and sending a brief burst of heat

59

outward. "So if you don't mind, now that I've seen the start of this adventure, I'll stay with you and see the end of it as well."

Then he brightened a bit. "Besides, between here and Tarnsberg is the whole Wilderness of Lannad. If you plan to travel off the road, the wild beasts alone will make you glad of another hand."

"If you're sure . . ." Randal began hesitantly.

"I've been thinking about this for a long time," Nick said. "And after seeing you again, I'm not certain that I didn't make a mistake when I left off studying the Art. I haven't forgotten everything I learned at the Schola; when we get back to Tarnsberg, maybe I can take up where I left off."

"You'd make a fine wizard," Randal told him. "I'm sure the Regents would let you back in if you asked."

They sat by the fire awhile more. "Go to sleep," Randal said finally. "At least one of us should get some rest."

The night was clear and chilly, with a wind blowing through the trees. Randal sat alone, listening to the sighing leaves while he kept up the illusion that hid the camp. By midnight, the stars shone down from a sky empty of clouds, and the moon lit the clearing with light strong enough to cast a few pale and wavering shadows. Dagon, Lys, and Nick stirred restlessly in their sleep, as if troubled by disturbing dreams. Out near the tree line, a movement caught Randal's eye.

A man was approaching, coming alone and on foot out of the Wilderness of Lannad.

He was just a pale outline at first. But then the

figure grew closer, and Randal felt a chill even colder than the night wind strike through him like a knife.

*I know him,* Randal thought. The raised scar on his right hand throbbed, and he pressed his palms together to stop their trembling. He remembered the day he had gotten that scar—*the circle, and the demons coming to drink my blood, and only Laerg's ceremonial sword standing between me and death.*

The man came nearer. He crossed the line of the circle inscribed in the dirt, but the circle did not break. "May I sit beside you?" the man asked. "I've walked far this night, farther than I like to think."

Randal could only nod in dumb agreement, too frightened to say no.

The voice was the same. The eyes were the same. This golden-haired man in wizard's robes—Randal knew him. This was his teacher, the wizard Laerg, who with the help of demons had tried to kill all the magicians in the realm. This was Laerg, sitting on a stone, his arms clasped around his knees for warmth, his face haggard and gaunt, a stubble of beard on his previously clean-shaven jaw—Master Laerg, whom Randal had seen buried in Tarnsberg many months past.

Randal found his voice. "Would you care for something to eat, stranger?"

"No, although I thank you," the man replied. Randal noticed that he could see the trees on the other side of the clearing, mistily, through the man's body. "But surely an apprentice ought to know his old master?"

61

"I'm not your apprentice anymore," Randal said carefully. "I'm a journeyman. And you're dead."

*I remember the sword in my hand,* he thought, *and my own blood dripping down onto the floor of your study, and then the blade striking home.*

"A journeyman already? How gratifying." Laerg looked directly at Randal for the first time. "And yes, I know you killed me. Let me thank you for that: You stopped me from making a great mistake. And I forgive you, too—the pain was momentary, and I've learned so much since then."

"But . . . why are you here now?"

Laerg smiled. "Let us say that I feel some lingering concern for a promising apprentice."

*"Some lingering concern" . . . you made me a wizard, I'll give you that much. But you had your own reasons.*

"I'm not sure I trust you," he murmured aloud.

The ghost nodded, as if acknowledging a point made in one of the Schola's many debates. "I'll admit that our last meeting was scarcely the kind of thing to inspire confidence."

"Planning to sacrifice me to demons, you mean? Hardly. Take power in the kingdom, destroy the Schola—little things like that?" Randal's voice had risen as he spoke, and now it came close to breaking. "Master Laerg, why did you do it?"

"I am a man, as other men"—the ghost looked down at his semi-transparent self and gave a faint laugh—"or I was, anyway. I had all the usual weaknesses, but I didn't know it. Through them I let myself be used by forces that I didn't understand."

The ghost met Randal's eyes. "There's a lesson there for you, if you want to dig it out."

"Thanks for the thought." The sword cut across Randal's hand was aching badly now. He clenched his fist over the pain. "I've got a reminder that I can make mistakes. I carry it with me all the time, thanks to you. If you really are you. For all I know, you could be a demon in Laerg's form."

The ghost raised the shadow of a golden eyebrow. "Inside your own circle? No, Randal . . . believe me or not as you will, but I have only your good at heart."

"If you wish me well," said Randal slowly, "then tell me, what do you know about the object I carry?"

"The statue?" asked Laerg. "One thing I can tell you: Master Varnart never owned it."

"He told Dagon that he did."

The ghost shook his head and looked at Randal with what might almost have been fondness. "Randal, Randal—you were always so charmingly innocent. There are a hundred ways to convey an untruth without ever lying."

Laerg's voice took on an echo of the tone that Randal remembered from a hundred lectures back in Tarnsberg. "Suppose that Master Varnart called this Dagon to him," the ghost went on, "and said, 'Lord Fess has stolen property in his castle.' A true statement, as it happens. And then: 'In his treasury is a certain ivory carving.' Again true. Then, finally, 'Lord Fess has no right to it. Bring it to me, and you will be richly rewarded.' All these things are true, and who can blame Varnart if Dagon hears something more than what was said?"

The ghost paused. "I never played those games myself. A man must have his pride—and I had somewhat more than most."

Randal blushed in the dark, knowing that he himself had spoken just such half-truths to Dagon more than once. Still, he said nothing of that to Laerg, but only asked, "What else do you know about this statue?"

"That Varnart wants it, that it is magical—but those things you already know." The ghostly wizard rose to his feet and looked down at his former apprentice. "One thing more, Randal—that carving is a thing of evil. I speak as someone who knows more than a little about evil, and I tell you, that statue is dangerous. Death follows it, and luck deserts it."

The sky was graying to the east. The birds were waking in the trees. Randal was surprised by how fast the time had gone. "Can't you tell me more than that?" he asked.

"Daybreak draws near," said the ghost, "and I have a long journey ahead of me." Laerg was looking more transparent by the moment. His voice was faint, nothing more than a whisper in the wind. "Only one thing more. Be careful, for your friends' sakes. Being near you can be deadly."

Randal drew a deep breath, hoping to question the ghost further—but before he could speak, Laerg had departed, as had the mist, torn on the light breeze of morning.

# VI.
# Running

ONE BY ONE, the others awoke.

Lys was the first, coming awake with a violent start and reaching out immediately for her lute in its leather case, as if she feared to find it gone. She relaxed when she saw Randal.

"Looks like we're still alive after all," she said with relief. "But if that's what sleeping inside a magic circle is like, don't ask me to do it again. I had nightmares the whole time."

Dagon yawned and stretched. "So did I. I dreamed I got an honest job."

The mercenary picked up his sword from where it had lain beside him all night long, sheathed it, and buckled the swordbelt around his hips. Then he looked around the campsite with a satisfied expression and chuckled. "But there are no enemies in sight, which is worth a few bad dreams as far as I'm concerned. I have to hand it to you, wizard—when you promise, you deliver."

Randal swallowed an exhausted yawn of his own. "I'm glad you approve," he said dryly. "And

66

I'd trade my night for yours if I had the chance."

Nick was the last to wake, rousing slowly and rubbing his eyes to clear away the final traces of sleep. He blinked at Randal and said, "You look like death warmed over—how long did you have to keep the circle up?"

"It's still here. Can't you feel it?" said Randal, and added, in the Old Tongue, "*I had a dead man visit me during the night.*"

Nick looked at him more closely. "*In the circle?*"

"*Yes. A master wizard, the one I told you about.*"

"*I won't ask more,*" said Nick. Then he switched back to the common speech of Brecelande. "But it's not surprising that I had strange dreams."

"I think we all did," said Lys. Her dark blue eyes clouded over with memories. "I dreamed of the day I found my family all murdered by bandits, and me left alone to starve."

"Not a good dream to wake up on," agreed Nick soberly. "My own dreams weren't bad, just odd. I dreamed that your statue had come alive, Randy—I was in Alured's shop back in Cingestoun, and that same old woman came walking in the door as large as life."

"What did she want?" asked Randal sharply. He seemed to hear again Master Laerg's final warning. *The carving is a thing of evil. . . . Be careful, for your friends' sakes.*

Nick shook his head. "I don't know. I said to her, 'You look like you've come a long way,' and she said, 'From Widsegard on the Southern Sea.' Then I thought she was going to ask me for something,

67

but I woke before she could say anything more."

"Widsegard," repeated Randal. Other than Nicolas, he didn't know anyone who came from there. Once it had been part of Brecelande, but after the High King's death, the city merchants had shut the gates and raised their own banner. "I wonder . . . was the statue made there in the first place?"

"Possibly," said Nick. "I thought the carving looked like southern work."

"What does it matter?" Dagon demanded. "It's here now."

Randal thought for a moment and turned to the mercenary. "Tell me," he said, "are you still determined to hand over the statue to Varnart?"

"Master Varnart and I had a bargain," said Dagon. "And he went back on it. Nobody gets the chance to cross me twice."

"And we've seen how dearly Fess's henchmen love us," said Lys. She looked at the young wizard. "What are you thinking, Randy? What should we do with that thing?"

Dagon grunted. "Drop it in a well, like you said yesterday, if I can't find a buyer for it in a hurry."

"No," said Randal. "I have a better idea. We can take it to Tarnsberg. The School of Wizardry is there, and maybe the masters can tell us what kind of thing we have."

*And besides,* he added to himself, *evil things don't stay down. If we threw that carving into a well, it would only crawl out again and do harm somewhere else.*

Dagon was frowning. "More wizards? I don't like

it. But I can't stay here, whatever I do. If I'm going to run, I might as well head for Tarnsberg and try to sell the statue there."

He cast a penetrating glance at Randal. "I suppose you'll want to keep on carrying the thing yourself?"

Randal nodded. "That's right." The young wizard was uncomfortably aware that he was working with partial truths again, but something about dealing with Dagon seemed to call them forth. *If this thing is really an artifact of power, then it's too dangerous to abandon—and too dangerous to sell.*

Once again Laerg's warning echoed in his mind— *be careful, for your friends' sakes*—and he turned to Lys and Nick. "Cingestoun isn't healthy for either of you right now, but once you're not with me and Dagon, you should be able to make it to Castle Doun. Lord Alyen is my uncle and a good man. Ask him for refuge. You'll be safe there."

Lys and Nicolas exchanged glances. Nick spoke first. "I'll stick with you," he said.

"I don't think you should do that," said Randal uneasily. "The statue is dangerous, and I don't want you and Lys to get hurt."

"What kind of friend would I be," Nick asked, "if I ran out on you when the trouble started? Like I said last night, I'm coming with you."

"I see," said Randal. He still didn't feel right about Nick's insistence on coming along, but the former apprentice's jaw was set in a stubborn line. Randal turned to the lute-player. "How about you, Lys?"

"Tarnsberg was as much my home as anywhere," she said. "I'll be glad to see it again. And you need somebody with common sense to keep you out of trouble."

Randal sighed. "Tarnsberg for all of us, then. Let's get out of here before Fess's men come back."

The four of them remounted Alured's carthorses and rode out. But Randal's words turned out to be prophetic. No sooner had they crossed the perimeter of the magic circle than a band of horsemen in yellow surcoats burst out of the trees and charged toward them.

"Ambush!" Dagon shouted. "Move out!"

The mercenary had his sword ready and was riding hard for a gap in the ring of horsemen, heading for the trees that marked the edge of the Wilderness. He didn't wait to see if anyone was following him.

*Fess's men,* thought Randal. *They must have surrounded the spot where our tracks vanished and then waited until morning to see what happened.*

He looked around for the others. Dagon had already disappeared into the trees, and Nick had almost reached shelter as well. But Lys hadn't yet won free of the clearing—and a pair of Fess's riders was closing in on her.

Randal gestured to call forth the flashing lights and booming thunder that could panic both men and horses. But Fess had trained his troopers well—they faltered but didn't stop.

Their brief confusion, however, allowed Lys to slip away into the trees. Randal turned to fend for himself. He threw a shock spell at a nearby rider, and the man tumbled from his horse. Randal kicked his own horse into a gallop and headed for the woods. The forest closed around him, but he could hear the sound of hoofbeats in pursuit.

*I have to slow them down,* Randal thought. *The only reason we just got away is because we rested our horses last night and they didn't.*

A spell of tangling and confusion would do the trick—but he had never cast such a spell before on his own, and the long watch over the magic circle had already left him drained. Once again, he became aware of the statue's power.

*Use me,* it seemed to say. *Use me, and become mightier than you have ever dreamed.*

"I don't want your power," he muttered aloud, "but if I don't use you, Fess's men will catch us all."

He brought the carthorse to a halt and began the spell. This time he was ready for the unpleasant surge of energy and directed it all into a maze of confusing tracks and deceptive images that Fess's men would find if they followed him into the woods.

"*Fiat!*" he cried, and the spell was ended. Then the backlash of power took him, and he collapsed onto his horse's neck, clutching the coarse mane in his hands.

Although the spell had weakened him, Randal found that drawing on the statue's power hadn't disgusted him as much as it had the last time. *I must be careful,* he thought, *and not use it unless I have to. I might get to liking it.*

After a moment, he straightened and rode on. It wasn't long before he saw Lys and Nick waiting among the trees ahead. He shook his head to clear

71

away the fog that casting the spell had left behind and asked, "Where's Dagon?"

"Don't know," said Nick. "But I'd guess he saved his own skin—he certainly took off fast enough."

"So did you all," said Dagon, riding up from behind them. "And you've been so noisy since then that I'm amazed we're not all crow's meat by now. Maybe I'd have more luck if I took that statue myself and left you to your own devices."

"I don't think so," said Randal wearily. "The spell of confusion I put on our trail will last until noon or so. That gives us a good head start if Fess's men want to follow us through the Wilderness."

They pushed on hard the rest of the day, always fearful that Fess's men would overtake them again. Night was falling before they paused.

"I figure we have half a day's lead on them," said Nick.

"Maybe," said Dagon. "And maybe not. In the meantime, we're in a horse race to Tarnsberg." He looked over at Randal. "Will the city take you in?"

"The Schola has to," said Randal. He swallowed what would have been a jaw-cracking yawn. The carthorse's jolting gait had given him no chance to rest all day, and he felt tired in his very bones. "And Tarnsberg is a free city. Its Council won't hand us over to a baron's riders, no matter how powerful Lord Fess may be around Cingestoun."

"Good," said Dagon. "Then let's concentrate on not losing our way."

Darkness fell suddenly in the woods, and they camped that night without a fire. When the first gray light came trickling through the thick foliage above, they rose and rode on.

Each day seemed the same, after that. They searched rivers for fords. They went around the heavier brush, or through it if need be. For several days they passed through craggy land, took shelter in caves, and never saw other living men.

"Do you suppose they're still following us?" Lys asked one evening as they sat beside a small stream that fell bubbling over the broken rocks.

"We can't afford to think they aren't," said Dagon. The mercenary was using his dagger to whittle a trap from a bit of broken wood. Every evening since they had entered the Wilderness, they had set out such snares, so that each morning brought them meat for the coming day.

Randal listened to the conversation without taking part. Once again, the day's riding had left him weak and shaken. His skin was hot and dry, and his head felt like it belonged to someone else. He sat leaning against a tree at the edge of the campsite, with his forehead resting on his upraised knees.

*I'm glad I don't have to do magic,* he thought. *I don't think I have the strength to work a single spell.*

After a while, Nick came over and sat beside him.

"Are you feeling well?" Nick asked.

"No," Randal answered, without lifting his head.

"I didn't think so," said the former apprentice. "If you want to know what I think, *I* think that statue is draining you somehow. You've looked pale and tired ever since you started carrying it around with you."

"Maybe," said Randal. The thought was a disturb-

73

ing one. *Did the statue kill Bryce?* he wondered. *Did it take all his magic and then leave him empty? Is that what it's doing to me?* He shivered, feeling suddenly fearful. "We have to get to Tarnsberg as fast as we can," he said aloud.

Lys joined them in time to overhear the last few words of their conversation. "Just when are we going to reach Tarnsberg, anyway?" she asked. "We've been wandering in these gloomy woods for a long time, with no sign of breaking out on the far side."

Randal looked up at the sound of Dagon's deep-voiced chuckle from the other side of the little camp. "I've got bad news for all of you," said the mercenary. "We aren't going to Tarnsberg."

Nick turned to glare at Dagon. "What do you mean?"

"We've been heading through the forest from north to south," said Dagon, "not east to west." The mercenary looked at the others. "Haven't you seen the slant of the sunlight? Haven't you noticed how each detour forces us southward?"

Lys had her hand on her dagger. "You didn't mention any of this before."

"If you weren't complaining, I wasn't going to stop you." The mercenary chuckled again. "That piece of ivory will bring a far better price from the merchant princes of the south." He went back to his work, still laughing to himself.

Nick, Lys, and Randal glanced at one another. "If we've been heading southward," said Lys, after a long pause, "then we're probably coming up to Widsegard."

"Then my dream about the old woman—" began Nick.

"—may not have been just a dream," Randal finished for him. "Few dreams are, after all."

"But what does it all mean?" asked Lys. "The dreams and the confusion?"

"I don't know," said Randal. "That's why I want to find a master wizard. This statue has too many puzzles wrapped around it for my liking."

"Why don't you put some kind of protection spell on it?" suggested Nick. "If it really is an artifact of power from somewhere around Widsegard, it could have been influencing our footsteps all this time."

Randal nodded slowly. "That's a good idea. If anybody's been tracing us by magic, the spell will make us harder to follow as well."

*But a protection spell is something I should have thought of a long time before this,* he reflected to himself. *Maybe the statue really has been working on me, like Nick said.*

Later that evening, after a scanty supper of rabbit grilled on sticks over a small campfire, Randal went off a little way into the forest. Kneeling on the mossy ground, he called up a pale cold-flame and then took the statue out of its leather bag. He looked at the carved figure by the witchfire's flickering light and once again felt certain that the figure had shifted its position. Perhaps the old woman's hand was a bit lower on her staff, or her mouth was a bit more open—he couldn't tell.

He put the statue down on the ground and traced a circle around it with a twig he'd broken from a nearby tree. He frowned for a moment in concentration and then wrote in the proper mystic signs at the four directions.

As he did so, the fog in his mind cleared for a moment, and he realized something. *Dagon was right: We've been traveling southward all along. The statue—or something—has been blurring our sense of direction.*

Quickly, while his mind was still clear, Randal began his conjuration. The spell was hard to work, even harder than he'd thought it would be. His head felt stuffed with rags, so that he could hardly remember the words, and he could feel the power in the statue wriggling and twisting as it tried to keep a way open to the outside world.

But at last the circle gave a flash of blue, and the spell was complete. He turned his attention to the bag, speaking the words that would turn it into a magical bag of holding to contain the power of the artifact. This spell slipped into place much more easily, and he realized that this wasn't the first time such a spell had been placed on the bag.

*Who broke the spell before, and what became of him?* Randal wondered. *Was it Bryce?*

But there wasn't any time to think about that now—he had to finish his work while the spell on the statue itself was still fresh. Moving rapidly, he picked up the statue and placed it in the bag. Then he pulled the leather drawstrings tight and tied the bag shut, sealing the knot with the words of binding.

For a moment he doubted that the spell had taken—the words were in his spell book, copied down during a long-ago lecture, but he had never before tried them in the real world. Now, though, it seemed to him that the bag pulsed with the energy it contained.

"Did you put the spell on it?" Nick asked when Randal walked back into the camp, carrying the bag in his hand. Nicolas and Lys were alone there, while Dagon was out placing his snares for tomorrow's meat.

"I did," said Randal, "as much as I could, anyway. I don't believe I'd have had any luck at all if the bag hadn't already been marked with magic. But the statue's power is contained now, as long as no one opens the bag."

The next day, they came to the first signs of human habitation they had found in weeks, and by evening they broke out of the Wilderness entirely. And just as Dagon had predicted, they emerged on the southern border of Brecelande—a region so far removed from the center of the kingdom that most people no longer considered themselves to be from Brecelande at all, but gave their loyalty to the nearest town or city, after the manner of the people of the far south.

"Not a healthy place to be," Nick commented. "The people here may not be loyal to Lord Fess, but they certainly aren't friendly to us. The threat of a blow or the promise of silver will get us handed over to anyone who asks."

"On the other hand," Randal said, "the people here aren't likely to be in Varnart's pay—and when we find Widsegard we'll find a Wizards' Guild as well. It's not the same as going back to the Schola, but at least it'll have some master wizards who can give us help."

They camped for the night at the edge of the forest and in the morning continued on, hoping to keep ahead of the pursuit they weren't certain still existed. Late in the afternoon of the second day, they came to the crest of a hill overlooking the ocean. At the edge of the blue water, golden towers sparkled in the low sunlight, and Randal looked down in wonder at the largest city he had ever seen.

# VII.
# Widsegard

WIDSEGARD WAS LARGER than Tarnsberg, larger than Tattinham in the eastern mountains, larger even than Cingestoun. The city walls were high and long, and colorful banners floated from the towers and gatehouses. Buildings inside the city took on the color of burnished gold in the light of the setting sun, and the roads coming and going were crowded with travelers on foot and on horseback, and with the wagons of merchants. Armed guards stood on the parapets, and the dying sunlight flashed from their polished spearpoints.

"Well," said Nick at last. "There it is. Do we go in?"

"I don't think we have much choice," said Randal. "I'm afraid we were meant to come here from the first. And that worries me."

"Then onward," said Dagon, with a laugh.

When they rode through the gates of Widsegard, the opening in the city wall above them was ten times the height of a man, with battlements on top and towers on each side. The road was so wide that even though they were riding four abreast, none of them rode next to the wall. More travelers, on horseback and on foot, filled the road on either side.

The guards at the gate didn't bother to stop them. Randal looked at the guardsmen curiously, realizing that these were fighting men of a far different stripe than the city guard back at Cingestoun. These were sturdy men, armored in mail and carrying long swords or huge double-bladed axes. They had an air of easy confidence about them, as if to say, "We are the law here, traveler, and no one challenges the law."

The four companions rode on into the city itself. Once they were past the walls, Randal asked Nick about the guardsmen at the gate.

"The city merchants pay them," Nick explained. "And with all the gold Widsegard earns from the southern trade, the city can afford to hire the best fighting men available."

They went on, riding between buildings of stuccoed brick and whitewashed stone. Shops with striped awnings spilled out their wares into booths and baskets that covered half the street. The scent of spices filled the air, the sweetness of cinnamon blending with the bite of pepper and the muskiness of sandalwood.

"One thing about a place like this," Lys said. "We're lost in the crowd."

"I wouldn't bet on that," said Dagon. "There are people in any town who earn their living trading answers for gold. Questions like, 'Did four northerners arrive the day before yesterday, and if so, where are they now?' are their daily bread."

As night fell around them, Lys saw an inn on the right. "I'm tired," she said. "Can't we rest?"

"This is as good a place as any," Randal replied. He swung down from his horse and went in. He found the innkeeper, a stocky, dour-faced man, and drew him aside.

"I'm interested in trading work for a room," said Randal. "Do you have any little problems you need taken care of—fleas in the bedding, weevils in the flour?"

The innkeeper scowled. "I run a clean inn without any wizard's tricks. You'll have to pay in coin like anyone else."

Randal didn't argue, although a room for the four of them cost him all the pennies remaining from his time in Cingestoun. "Money well spent," was Lys's comment, when Randal came out to tell them the news. "This isn't the sort of town where you can sleep out on the street."

Somewhere nearby, somebody was frying something in hot oil—Randal could hear the oil crackling and caught the odor of cooking meat coming to him through the other city smells of garbage, spices, and sweat. He realized that he felt truly hungry for the first time since he'd taken the statue from Bryce, back at the Green Bough.

"Is there any way we can get some food?" he asked.

"I've got a coin or two," Dagon offered. "I'll stable the horses and be back soon."

The other three went up to the room in the inn. Despite the innkeeper's words to Randal, it was small, dark, and dirty. "I think you got robbed of those coppers," Nick said as they looked over the sleeping space.

"It's only for one night, and I can make it better," Randal answered as he set about the preparations to send the assorted vermin elsewhere and clear a bit of the reek from the air. Lys and Nick watched him as he worked.

For Randal, the use of such simple, honest magic felt good. He had been doing nothing but hurting and hiding for much too long. "Even if this is your old home city," he said to Nick as he finished the spells, "let's do what we came to do and then move on."

"And just what *did* you come here to do?" asked Dagon, entering the room with a loaf of bread and a basket of meat in his hands. "I came here to get some money for that cursed ivory statue you've been cuddling like a baby ever since we left Cingestoun."

"I'm looking for a master wizard," said Randal. "Or a library of the Art, or a Wizards' Guild of some kind . . . because 'cursed' is a good word for that statue, and it's more than I can handle alone. Tomorrow I'll go looking for the place, and by evening I should have an answer."

"I hope you do," said Dagon. "I'm a man of patience, but not very great patience. I have my own business to transact."

They soon turned in, but Randal was unable to sleep. The others were restless as well, and once, Lys cried out from the midst of some nightmare. Nick lay on his pallet as if he were turned to stone, and sweat glistened on his forehead.

In the morning, they arose. The day was clear, but the air was heavy and oppressive with the late-summer heat.

"We'll have a storm before tomorrow, if I'm not mistaken," said Nick, glancing out the window at the sky. "We'd better take care of our business before it breaks. It's been a long time since I lived here—and I was just a boy when I left—but I think I can find the Wizards' Guildhall without getting lost."

Randal swallowed the last of a bit of bread left over from the evening before. "Then let's go."

"I'm coming, too," Lys said. "I wouldn't mind seeing a bit of Widsegard with somebody who knows where things are."

"Well, I'll stay here," said Dagon. "I'm not the one who's hunting for wizards." The mercenary gave the other three a hard look. "Just remember, if you don't come back, the horses are mine."

As soon as Randal was outside with Lys and Nick, he turned to his friends and said, "Let's get on with it. The sooner I can find a master wizard, the better —I'll hand over the statue, and it can be somebody else's problem from then on."

"I don't know," Nick said. "Our friend Dagon seems to think the statue is his to dispose of."

"Only because he stole it for Varnart," said Randal. "Or hired Bryce to steal it for Varnart, since Bryce was at least gutter-trained in wizardry and Dagon hasn't drawn a magical breath in his entire life. But the statue wasn't Varnart's any more than it was Fess's, and it isn't Dagon's."

"It's not yours, either, if it comes to that," Nick

pointed out. "But I suppose someone has to see that it's taken care of." The former apprentice shook his head. "Somehow, I don't think that Alured will be seeing me or his horses again. I'll have to find a way to make it up to him."

The three walked through the streets, searching for the Wizards' Guild. But the city had changed since Nick's childhood, and few of the landmarks from his memories matched reality any longer. As the morning wore on, the three travelers were reduced to asking passersby where the Guildhall might be.

"Randy," Nick said, after one such conversation, "have you noticed anything strange about how people have been looking at us in the street?"

Now that Nick had mentioned it, Randal realized that there was indeed something odd going on. In other parts of Brecelande, the loose black wizard's robe he wore over his ordinary clothing gained him respect and even a measure of protection—Dagon, Randal felt certain, would have cut his throat in a heartbeat without it. But here, the expressions he saw as he walked past were different. Some people looked curious, some alarmed, and a few even made hand signs against the evil eye and other sinister enchantments.

*Something very strange is going on in this city,* he thought. *Something to do with magic.*

The sun was a pale, hot disk high overhead before they found the Guild: a white-plastered building on one side of an open square. The windows on both floors were covered by painted wooden shutters, and the heavy door was closed.

"That's the Wizards' Guildhall, all right," Nick said. "But it looks different. Something's wrong."

Something was indeed wrong. The whole place had an air of decay about it—the whitewashed walls had faded, and the paint on the shutters was peeling away. When Randal went closer, he saw that the door had been nailed shut with iron spikes. The spikes were rusty, and spiders had spun their webs around the doorjamb.

He walked back to his two companions, and the three of them retired to the other side of the square. They stood in the shadow of another stone building and looked across at the deserted Guildhall.

"Now what?" Nick asked.

"Guardsmen coming up the street," Lys said quietly, before Randal could answer. "Both directions."

Then, in carrying tones, she shrieked, "How *dare* you suggest such a thing! I'm a good girl!" and with her left hand slapped Randal so hard across the cheek that his head rang. At the same time, he felt the dagger in her right hand cutting the leather cord that tied the statue's protective bag to his belt. Before he could protest, Lys was gone, blending into the gathering crowd as a dozen guardsmen converged on the plaza.

Randal hardly had time to wonder what was going on before he found himself surrounded by guardsmen, their swords all drawn and pointed at him and Nick.

"Not a word, wizard," said the captain of the guards. "Don't try to get away. You're coming along with us."

Randal looked at Nick and shrugged.

*I could run,* thought Randal. *But I wouldn't get very far—the captain's wearing an amulet just like the one Varnart's man wore at the tower. My spells wouldn't work on him. I wish I knew what Lys was up to. . . .*

He decided to put as good a face on things as possible and made a respectful bow to the captain of the guards. "My friend and I are at your service, sir."

The captain wasn't impressed. "Very pretty," he said. He nodded at one of his troop. "Search them, Freki." To Randal, he said, "Try anything on my man, wizard, and you're both dead where you stand."

The guard called Freki searched both Nick and Randal—taking their eating knives and Randal's spell book. Randal knew better than to protest as he saw the fruit of three long years of study handed over to the captain. Just the same, he winced inwardly as the captain leafed through the painstakingly inscribed pages and snorted, "Looks like wizard stuff to me. Maybe someone at the guardhouse will be able to read it."

The captain handed the book to Freki with a curt "Keep this for evidence," and then turned back to Nick and Randal. "You two come along."

The guards marched the two northerners through the streets of Widsegard to a huge, bleak stone building with more of the city guards standing watch at the gate and lounging around the courtyard within. The captain and Freki escorted Randal and Nick across the courtyard and up a flight of stone steps to a small room where another guardsman—this one older, with gray in his hair and beard—sat behind a wooden desk. The guard at the desk looked Randal and Nick up and down.

"What do we have? Public brawling?" the older man asked.

"No, sir," said the captain. "Show him the evidence, Freki."

Freki laid Randal's spell book on the desk. The older guard picked it up.

" 'Randal of Doun,' " he read aloud. He looked at the young wizard. "That you?"

Randal nodded. "Yes."

"We've had more than enough trouble with your kind. Possession of magical books or implements gets you a flogging through the city gates."

Randal didn't say anything. The older guard nodded to the captain. The captain turned to Freki and said, "Lock 'em up."

Freki nodded in turn and marched the two northerners out of the small room and down into the depths of the prison. They came to an underground cell, dark and foul-smelling and cold in spite of the warm air in the world outside. An iron grille barred the entrance to the cell. Freki unlocked the door and pulled it open. "In there," he said.

Randal and Nick obeyed, and the door clanged shut. Freki locked it and strode away down the dim corridor.

"Well," said Nick, after a long pause. "What do you think our chances are of breaking out of here before morning?"

Randal moved over to the damp wall of the cell and sank tiredly down onto the dirty straw that covered the stone floor. "We can't," he said. "I can feel spells of binding on this place that go back for centuries."

He leaned his head against the wall and closed his eyes. The sense of increased well-being that he'd felt since putting the statue and its bag into a protective binding had begun to ebb away, bringing back the dragging exhaustion that had beset him on the road from Cingestoun.

*The spell wasn't broken completely when Lys cut the drawstring,* he thought blearily, *but it must have been weakened. That's why I feel this way—the statue's feeding on my lifeforce. At this rate, I may not live long enough to see what kind of justice Widsegard has for wizards. I hope Lys can find somebody who can deal with that artifact. It's dangerous, and it's starting to work its way loose.*

He heard Nick saying something close by, but he was suddenly too weary to answer. With his cheek resting against the cold stone, he fell asleep.

Randal woke with a start and stared around. Nothing had altered, it seemed—nothing had happened to account for his waking. He stood up and stretched. The weariness he'd felt before was gone, and he turned back toward the wall to give Nick a hand up onto his feet.

Two skeletons lay on the floor of the cell. The disconnected bones of the closer one were covered by a loose black robe. A wizard's robe.

Randal bit back a cry of fear. Carefully, he raised his own arm, still clad in the wide black sleeve of his Schola robe, and touched his own flesh. *Solid,* he thought. *Warm. I'm alive, and this is a dream. But where is Nick?*

"Nick?" he whispered. "Are you here, too?" But no answer came to him, and the two skeletons grinned in silent mockery.

Randal felt a slight breeze pass through the dungeon corridor, bending the flames of the smoky torches set in brackets outside the cells. *Someone must have opened a door somewhere,* he thought. *If they have doors in dreams.*

Then he heard a sound. The light tap-tap-tap of someone walking, walking with a cane or a staff. Under his robe, Randal felt sweat trickle down his back.

Panic seized him. Whoever was coming, he knew, was coming for him. And there was nowhere to hide down here, nowhere to run to. He grabbed the bars of the door and shook them, but the door didn't budge. A shadow was growing visible in the passageway leading to the cell, a shadow walking slowly.

Then the figure came into view—an old woman, garbed in a long white cloak, with strands of gray hair floating from under the hood. In her hand she clasped the staff on which she leaned.

She walked up to the door of the cell, her staff tapping with each step she took. When Randal looked at her face, he could tell that she was blind: White film covered both her eyes. Randal recognized the old woman—she was the statue he had carried over mountain and moor from Cingestoun, grown to human size and brought to horrible life.

The woman faced in his direction and spoke. "Set me free," she said.

"How can I?" Randal asked. "I'm the one in prison, not you."

Then, abruptly, Randal saw that he was wrong. He was looking in through the door of a cell, not out as he had thought, and the woman was standing in the cubicle. Randal felt something cold in his hand. It was a ring of keys.

"Don't worry, granny, I'll help you," he heard himself saying. Even as he spoke, he was trying keys in the lock. He found one that fit and turned it. With a howl of rusting metal, the bolt withdrew. Randal pulled the door open. "You can come out now."

The old woman took a step forward. "Take me with you. I have to find my way home."

"Come on, take my arm," Randal said. "We'll get out together."

Slowly they walked up the passageway, turned, and took the stairway up. At last they came to the small room that topped the dungeons. The light of the setting sun slanted in through the window, illuminating motes of dust with gold and smearing red light on the walls. The room had guardsmen in it, and they moved, and they talked, but no sound came from their mouths. Still, Randal knew that he hadn't gone deaf—he could hear the buzzing of a single fly and, farther off, the breaking of the waves on the cliffs under the city's walls.

His spell book still lay on the wooden desk. Unnoticed by the guards, he picked it up and put it into the deep pocket of his wizard's robe. Then he went on, the old woman pacing slowly by his side, her hand holding on to his upper arm with a grip so

91

hard that it was painful. The staff went tapping before her, a steady, relentless sound.

People thronged the streets of the city, but still no one saw Randal and the old woman, though the path opened before them, as if by chance. They walked through the gaps, and the crowd closed behind them again.

Randal and the old woman continued on. At last, they faced a set of wide steps leading to the walls of the sea side of the city. *Who's guiding whom?* Randal asked himself. *Where is she taking me?*

They came to the top of the wall, the setting sun a burning orb of blood red balanced on the horizon.

The old woman turned to Randal. "If you truly wish to follow me," she said, "you will throw yourself into the sea."

*She thinks I'm one of her worshippers!* Randal thought. The daze that held him broke, and he wrenched his arm out of her grasp. "No!"

"Thousands before you were honored to perform lesser acts," the woman said softly.

She raised her hand, and Randal felt a fascination with the edge of the parapet. It would be nice to stand up there. And the sea, where it rushed over the rocks a hundred feet below, looked cool and refreshing. He felt hot and sticky, and his body itched after sleeping on the prison's filthy straw. A swim would be so nice. . . .

"No!" he shouted again, and tore his gaze away from the tempting water.

He turned back to the old woman leaning on her

staff, and he cast the spell of clear seeing, to look beyond illusion and see the truth.

The woman looked the same as before. No . . . wait . . . now she was younger than he had thought, not much older than he was himself, and the long cloak was a bridal gown. She beckoned to Randal and smiled.

"No," Randal said, "I'm not going to go where you lead. Your way is death."

She reached out a hand and clenched it. Randal felt a pain in his chest, as if his heart was being pulled out of his body. Desperately, he cast a shield spell, and the pain faded. Then he tried a shock spell, to knock her away from him, but the enchantment went wild and turned into a green mist between them that made it difficult to see beyond the little patch of stone wall where they stood.

The girl came closer and closer still. "Come with me," she said. She reached out and touched Randal's shoulder. He flinched away.

Then he awoke.

"Come with me," Lys said, kneeling over him, shaking his shoulder. "Come with me. We've got to get out of here."

# VIII.
## Bargains

"COME ON," said Dagon, from the open doorway of the cell. "Nobody stays bribed forever."

Randal rose to his feet. The dungeon had chilled him through and left him aching in every joint. Moving hurt. *I feel old,* he thought. *If I'd stayed home in Doun I'd still be only a squire in my uncle's castle. Instead, I'm escaping from a southlands prison, and I feel like I'm a thousand years old.*

Lys hustled him and Nick out through the door. Randal glanced at her belt as he passed. "Where's the statue?"

"Shh!" Lys said. "It's safe. Let's get out of here."

They hurried through a maze of twisted passage-ways, all leading down. Randal could hear Dagon counting the turnings to himself. At last, they emerged through a narrow slit of a door opening onto a dark, narrow street. Far above, Randal could see a faint sprinkling of stars.

All right," said Nick. "Let's go someplace where the city guard won't come by in the next minute, and sort this out."

A few minutes later, the four companions were sitting around a squalid room in one of Widsegard's dirty waterfront inns. Dagon had slid the bolt home behind them as they entered, and now he leaned by the wall to one side of the door.

Randal looked about and shook his head without speaking.

"Well," said Lys, "Nick asked for a place where the guard stayed out, and this part of town looks like it."

"I'm not surprised," said Randal finally. "How are we paying for it?" He gestured at the smoke-stained walls. "It's not much, but I've spent all my money already."

He reached into the pocket of his robe, intending to turn it inside out to demonstrate his penniless state. His fingers brushed against the coolness of leather. It was his spell book. The one the guards had taken from him.

"What's wrong, Randy?" asked Lys. "You look funny."

"You spend a night in jail and see how you look afterward," he answered. The book had been taken from him and not returned by the guards—and despite his dream, he hadn't been out of the cell until Lys arrived. But someone, somehow, wanted him to have the book.

*The statue,* he thought. *That has to be it. It wants me to keep on acting as a wizard. It wants me to use my powers.*

"Got fleas from the dungeon, I suspect," said Dagon with a knowing expression. "It happens every time."

"You still haven't mentioned where you came by the money for this room," Nick said. "Let alone for a bribe."

"Pawned my lucky sapphire again to save you, out of a spirit of fellowship." Dagon grinned at Nick. "We wound up selling the horses, too. Sorry." Nick glowered at Dagon, but the mercenary didn't seem particularly upset.

Randal had listened to the talk with only half an ear. Now he turned to Lys. "By any chance did you manage to learn what's happened in Widsegard to make wizards so unwelcome?"

"I heard stories," she said. "For starters, about three or four years ago, the city merchants threw all the wizards out of town."

"And they just left," said Dagon. "So much for the power of wizardry."

"No," said Randal. "They'd leave if the city told them to go. Staying where we aren't welcome isn't worth destroying a city for."

Lys nodded, her face grim. "The head of the Wizards' Guild told the city merchants something like that when he got the order."

Nick scratched his curly brown beard. "A bunch of merchants wouldn't do a thing like that without a reason," he said. "I learned that much, working in Cingestoun. What had the wizards been doing to start the trouble?"

*Wizards wouldn't . . .* Randal's thought began, and then he stopped. *By now, you know for yourself that a wizard is just as capable of villainy as anybody else.*

Lys and Dagon exchanged glances. "That's where

96

people start getting real quiet," said the mercenary. "Nobody wants to name names . . . but I get the impression that Widsegard had a full-scale war going between two rival groups of magicians for control of the Wizards' Guild."

"The City Council left them alone at first," Lys explained, "mostly because the merchants weren't sure which side to back. All the Schola-trained wizards were on one side—but the other wizards belonged to a tradition that grew up in Widsegard years before the Schola was ever founded."

"So the Council stood by and let them fight it out for a while," finished Dagon, "but when ordinary people started getting killed, the Council threw out the whole Guild instead of picking one side over the other. And wizardry's been illegal in Widsegard ever since."

Randal felt a sudden cold stillness in the center of his bones. "But what if one side never really left?" he whispered. "If they could get their hands on an artifact of power—one from this city, even—and summon it home by magic from whatever strong-room happened to hold it, then they could control the whole city and not just the Guild."

He shivered. "We have to get back north to Tarns-berg," he said. "The longer that statue stays in Widsegard, the worse everything becomes."

"Don't worry," said Lys. "We're sneaking out by the Ragpickers' Gate as soon as I go fetch that leather bag from where I hid it."

"Is it somewhere safe?" Randal asked.

"Safer than carrying it around would be."

"And she wouldn't tell me where it was," Dagon put in, "unless I agreed to help get you out of jail." From the sound of the mercenary's voice, he might have been either irritated or somewhat amused.

For a little while, there was silence. The heat of the day had not yet faded from the tiny room. Randal stood and walked to the window for a breath of air to clear the lingering dungeon smell from his nostrils.

The room overlooked the harbor, and the low-hanging moon blazed a silver path across the bay. Above the port district, the cliffs rose sheer, crowned at their summit by the walls of the main city above. Long breakwaters stretched out from the cliffs into the deep, and ships lined the edges of the harbor. On the end of one of the breakwaters was a light-house, a tower with a beacon fire that painted the harbor with a red glow.

The sky overhead was cloudless, but a low haze was rapidly gathering on the horizon. The ocean looked like a millpond, smooth but for the ripples showing on its glassy surface.

*If there is a storm brewing,* Randal thought, *we'd better get out of the city before it breaks.*

He looked down at the open square below, lit by moon and fire. Riding through the square, looking carefully to right and left, was a troop of horsemen in yellow livery: Lord Fess's men-at-arms, still searching for the four companions.

Randal beckoned to the others. "Trouble," he said, pointing to the riders below.

"I don't like the looks of this," Dagon said. "Don't they *ever* give up?"

"It seems we got out of prison just in time," Nick said. "If they're looking for a wizard in this town, that's the first place they'll check." He glanced over at Dagon. "We still have something to settle about those horses, but I have to thank you for saving our lives."

"Your lives aren't saved yet," Dagon pointed out.

"No," Lys said, "but this might just be our good luck. They'll spend weeks searching the city, and all the time we'll be on the road to Tarnsberg."

"We may have more trouble getting there than you think," said Randal slowly. "That statue brought us here. Powerful spells must have been cast to bring it home, and now that it's here it wants to stay. I don't know how much longer I can handle it—it has a feel of death to it, and a strength in it that needs a master wizard to control."

"Randy!" Nick exploded. "If I hear you wish one more time for a master wizard to come help you out, I'm going to hit you with a brick. You're the only wizard around here, and if magic is the problem and magic is the solution, then you're the only one who can handle it. Now, what are you going to do?"

Randal dropped his head into his hands. *Nick's right,* he thought. *That statue became my responsibility the minute I took it from Bryce. So now it's my job to decide what we do next.* He paused a moment longer to order his thoughts and then lifted his head again.

"First," he said, "I think we should get the statue from wherever Lys hid it. If dropping it down a well was a bad idea before, leaving it lying about in Widsegard is a worse idea now. So we'll have to take it with us when we go."

"If it will let us," Lys said. She gave a shaky laugh. "See—you've frightened me with your talk."

"You mean if *I'll* let you go," Dagon said. "I still want to sell that statue and buy back my lucky dagger."

The candle flickered in the room, sending the shadows dancing. Lys rose to her feet. "I'll go get the statue," she said. "Now's as good a time as any. We can be gone by daybreak."

"I'll go with you," said Randal. "This time you're the one needing someone to watch your back."

Lys didn't argue the point. She and Randal left the waterfront inn together, and Lys traced a path through the dark streets. The roads here in the port district all led uphill to the main city, and the steep climb left Randal panting. When they reached the point where the narrow road pierced the city wall, Lys stopped and turned to Randal.

"I have to do some climbing now," she said. "You'd better stay down here—you look done in."

Randal was too tired to protest. He nodded in agreement, and Lys disappeared silently into the shadows. He settled himself against the wall to wait.

Time passed, and Randal began to worry. *Lys has been gone a long time,* he thought. *Maybe too long.* His anxiety grew as the minutes went by and the lute-player failed to reappear. *I don't think she is coming back,* he said to himself in a panic. *Something's happened to her. And there's nobody to help her but me.*

He considered doing a scrying to find her, then shook his head. That idea was no good. There was nothing nearby for him to look in, and he had an increasing sensation that something was spreading strange magic through the night, like rings in a pool of water disturbed by a thrown rock, distorting all that it touched.

*I've got to get Nick,* he thought frantically, *and then we can both go find Lys.* He turned back downhill toward the waterfront, a plan already forming in his head. *We'll give Dagon what he wants—or give him something that looks like it for a little while, anyway—and then be rid of him. If he sold the horses, he's made a profit on the deal, and we don't owe him anything.*

Randal looked about for suitable objects on which to cast a spell of physical change, to produce an illusory replica of the missing statue. *When is an illusion a lie,* he wondered, *and when is it not?* At the Schola, those had been topics for scholarly debate among the student wizards—now the practical aspects were looming before him. *If I lie, I am no wizard, and my magic will never be trustworthy again.*

Randal was nearing the waterfront inn. And there he found what he needed: a torn and dirty burlap sack and a piece of rotten fruit, discarded from one of the merchant's stalls. He placed the fruit—a peach, from the fuzzy skin and sickly-sweet odor—into the sack and cast the spell of visual illusion. The bundle shifted and changed, taking the form and shape of the statue in its leather bag.

The effort of the spell left Randal even weaker than before. He was aware of the other, real statue somewhere in the city, a source of power calling out to him to be used. *The protection I've put on it is completely gone.* But this time he resisted the temptation to tap into that deep well of mystic energy. *Whatever I do, it must be my own effort now.*

Randal reached the inn and climbed the stairs to the dirty room. The local customs apparently included minding one's own business—no curious heads had turned as he passed through the crowded downstairs common room.

Upstairs, he knocked at the door and walked in. Before he could speak, Dagon gestured him into silence. "This man has a message," the mercenary said.

*This man?* Randal looked around the room. Nick was standing against the far wall, arms crossed on his broad chest and anger burning on his face. A small, gray man in greasy clothing stood beside the door.

"Good," the man said. "I see you have something with you. If it's what I think it is, you'll get the girl back again. Open the bag and let me look at it."

*I hope the illusion is good enough,* Randal thought. *The bad light will be a help.*

The young wizard reached into the sack of illusory leather and pulled out what appeared to be an ivory statue of an old woman. To Randal's eye it was only a crude copy, with none of the sinister life of the original. But maybe it would pass.

It did. "Ah, yes," the man said. "You don't know how long we've waited for her to come home. Bring it to the Crystalmen's Plaza at moonset, and we will trade the girl for that statue. Agreed?"

*How long should I pause, to seem real? Long enough, but not too long.*

"Agreed," Randal said at last.

"At moonset, then." The gray man gave a half-bow, slipped out the door, and vanished.

"What happened out there?" Nick asked after a moment of heavy silence. "How did they get Lys?"

Randal collapsed into the room's only chair. "She climbed up somewhere to get the statue," he said in dull tones. "Someone must have captured her."

"Someone indeed," said Dagon. "It's the wizards. Fess's men would be more direct—a charge up the stairs is their style. And this was a local man, not one of Varnart's litter. Looks like you were right: Someone here wants that piece of dead bone. And it seems as if wizards still aren't too finicky to hire people like me to do their dirty work."

"You can't give the statue to those people," Nick protested. "Think of the evil that will come of it."

"I won't be giving it to them," Randal replied. "I can't. This is only an illusion. I have no idea where the real statue is, except that it's still somewhere in the city."

He pushed himself to his feet and wearily made his way to the window. The moon was already descending into the clouds that hid the horizon. "We have to be on our way," he said. "Moonset is only a few minutes from now. Where is this Crystalmen's Plaza?"

"It's where all the glassmakers have their shops," Nick replied. "I think I know where it is."

"Then lead on."

Behind him, Randal could hear Dagon muttering. "More double-crosses. I don't like it."

Nick was able to find the plaza without too much trouble. Randal knew they were in the right place when he saw the shops of glassblowers and window- and mirror-makers gathered around a central square with a fountain. He took up a position near the fountain, with Nick and Dagon close behind him.

"Remember," Randal said, "whatever we do, the main thing is to get Lys back."

With the moon gone, the night had turned blacker, and heavy clouds had begun building up over the ocean. In the darkness, Randal saw Nick nod his head—a movement of shadow against shadow. "Here they come," said the carpenter.

The man from the inn room came up to them. "You have it?"

Randal held up the bag. "What you saw is still here."

The man gestured. Two other men came forward through the dark, holding a girl between them.

"Let the girl start walking toward us," Randal said. "When she gets halfway across, I'll toss you the bag."

The shadowy girl started to walk across the square. When she had come about halfway, Randal tossed the bag to the men who had released her. At the same time he called out, "Lys, run!"

The girl broke into a dash. As soon as she reached the waiting three, she collapsed against Randal. "Oh, Randy, am I glad to see you!"

"No time to talk," Nick said. "Let's go."

They ran. The four of them were a couple of streets and an alley away before they slowed.

"You sure fooled them with that fake," Dagon said to Randal. "Now let's get the real one."

"Lys?" Randal said.

"Yes, let's go do it. And then get out of this city."

Randal had his doubts about how possible that might be. The city guards would be looking for him, Fess's men had come to town and were looking for him, and now these others would be looking for him as well. Randal knew they wouldn't stay fooled long. No change spell lasts forever, and sooner or later the mock statue would return to being a rotten peach.

Lys led them to another part of town. Randal recognized the section of the city wall where he had lost her before, only this time they were approaching it from the other side. He watched as she climbed up a wooden drainpipe and retrieved something from where it had been jammed under a balcony. A bag.

"Is that it, this time?" Dagon asked.

"Yes," said Lys.

And Randal echoed, "Yes," as he took the bag. He could feel the magic of the statue reaching out to him through its protective shroud.

Suddenly, a sharp whistle sounded from the darkness. Lys cried out in alarm. Randal looked up and froze. Both ends of the alley were crowded with robed and hooded figures, all of them holding wicked, curving knives.

# IX.
# City Fight

THE LEADER OF the newcomers threw a leather purse down onto the pavement at Dagon's feet. Randal heard the clink of coins as it landed. As the mercenary bent to scoop it up, the other man called out, "See, we keep our bargains—here is the rest of your gold. Now hand over the real statue, as you promised."

*These must be the outlaw wizards,* Randal thought. *The ones who were calling the statue home.* He heard Lys gasp. "Dagon!" she exclaimed, making the mercenary's name sound like a curse. "Why did you do it?"

The mercenary turned to face her. "I kept telling you the statue was mine to sell," he said. "And I needed the money to buy back my dagger. Give the man the statue, like he said."

Randal felt his stomach churn. *All of our lives count for less with him than his blasted knife.* He looked in vain for some expression of remorse, or even of satisfaction, in Dagon's face—anything that would help him understand what had just happened. But the mercenary had already turned away.

The leader of the hooded strangers held out his hand to Randal. "Give me the statue, wizard, and we will let you leave unharmed."

"Randy," Lys muttered, "maybe you ought to . . ."

She never completed the sentence. Lightning flashed, and thunder boomed out—not magical thunder, but real thunder from the sky above. Another bolt of lightning followed closely, zigzagging down to strike one of the highest towers of Widsegard. Cold rain poured from the heavens. The storm that had been brewing all day had broken at last.

Over the sound of rain, Randal heard hoofbeats, loud and growing louder. Then there was an outcry from the mass of hooded men at one end of the alley, and a moment later a troop of horsemen, their swords drawn and ready, rounded the corner and burst in upon the hooded men at a gallop.

"Yellow surcoats!" Lys exclaimed. "Lord Fess's riders are attacking from the rear!"

*They must have been following the statue all this time,* thought Randal. With Nick and Lys, he flattened himself against one wall of the alley as horsemen in yellow surcoats fought hooded footmen in the teeming rain—a vicious, close-quarters combat pent up between the stone buildings that fronted the alley.

The three young people huddled, forgotten, against the wall. Sounds of fighting filled the night air—the clash of swords against curving knives, the harsh shouts of men in battle, the cries of the wounded. Where Dagon had gone to, or on which side he now fought, Randal couldn't tell. Then, above the noise of battle, a horn sounded.

"The city guard is coming out!" Nick shouted. "We can't let them catch us!"

A riderless horse bolted past, a coil of rope swinging wildly from the horn of the empty saddle. Nick made a grab for the horse's bridle and brought the frightened animal under control. "If we get a couple more of these," he said, "we can ride out of here."

"No," Randal said. "We'd never make it out through all the fighting. Give the rope to me, and let the horse go."

He took the loop of rope in his hands and uncoiled it. Then he dropped it onto the pavement at his feet and leaned back against the stone wall. He closed his eyes and searched deep within himself, seeking the strength to do what came next.

"Randy, are you all right?" Nick asked.

"I'm going to try something," he said, without opening his eyes. "Let Lys go first. She's the lightest."

Randal spoke the words and made the gestures of a levitation spell—one that he had last used in happier days, when he and the wizard Balpesh together had restored a ruined bridge. He reached far down into himself for the power to make the light rope uncoil and rise, snakelike, through the dark alongside the wall. It went up fast until it hung fully extended, its top lost in the stormy night.

"Lys," he said. "Go."

Lys grasped the hanging rope and pulled herself up, hand over hand. Acrobat that she was, she took no more than a minute to make the climb. A few seconds longer, and she called down, "I've got it! Nick, you're next."

Nick turned to Randal. "You look too tired to climb. When I get up, you tie the end around your waist, and Lys and I will pull you up."

Randal nodded and gestured to Nick to be on his way. The former apprentice grabbed the rope, set one boot against the wall, and half pulled himself up the rope, half walked up the wall. He was lost in the shadows above. Then his voice called down, "Randy! Tie on and let's go!"

Randal leaned against the wall a moment longer, then wrapped the end of the line around his waist and tied it in front of him. Reaching up, he tugged twice on the rope.

He went up the side of the wall in a quick series of yanks. Once, he swung, smashing into the stone, but he didn't lose consciousness or his grip on the rope. Soon he came to the edge of the roof, and eager hands grasped him and helped him over.

Randal lay for a moment on the slick clay roof tiles, breathing hard. The storm that had broken minutes earlier was raging now. Wild lightning ripped the sky apart, making the city as bright as day for a few seconds and then casting everything into darkness again. The rain plastered Randal's hair against his skull. The chilly droplets trickled down his neck and under his clothing, but he wasn't cold.

Instead, he burned with fever. *Nick was right, the same thing that got Bryce is getting to me,* he thought, but he was too tired to feel any emotion about the prospect. He wanted nothing more than to lie on the rooftop and let the storm wash over him—no more moving, no more problems.

Lys tapped him on the shoulder. "I've found an outside stairway leading down to the next street over," she said. "Let's get started before somebody figures out where we've gone."

Wearily, Randal rolled over onto his side and pulled himself to his feet. He swayed, and Nick caught him. Then, with Randal leaning on Nick's arm for support, they followed Lys down the outside stair. In the alley they paused, gasping for breath, while the rain still poured down.

"How many of them do you think there were?" Lys asked.

"I don't know," Randal replied. "How many followers does a master wizard have, if he can promise them a share in the power that a magical artifact can bring? Widsegard was wrong to throw out its wizards, I think—only the goods ones left."

They came to the mouth of the alley. Nick stepped out into the street, then jumped back as a bolt of magical lightning sizzled past in front of him. "That was close," he said. "They're out there waiting for us."

Randal gestured to Lys and Nick to move farther back. "Let me see what I can do," he said, and reached within himself to the dark place where his deepest reserves were stored. *I didn't know I had enough magic in me to do everything I've done tonight,* he thought. *Something is stretching in me . . . power responding to need, maybe. I'm not certain if it's going to save me or kill me—and right now I don't care.*

Gathering his energies together, Randal prepared a shield spell for protection, and an illusion of fog to blur their images. He threw the illusion in the area around the alley's entry, then put the shield spell on himself and his friends.

"Now let's go," he said. "Make for that alley over there."

They ran. A lightning bolt flashed out of the darkness toward them, but it bounced off the shield spell Randal had cast. As he ran, Randal threw a lightning bolt of his own in reply, but without a clear target the stroke went wild, splintering stone and gouging walls but doing no other damage. The three fugitives reached the other side of the street, then ducked down yet another alley.

"There are at least two of them still after us," said Lys.

"Randy," Nick whispered, "you'll have to do something stronger. They're trying to kill us."

"They're just trying to get us to drop the statue," Randal said in a ragged voice. He was exhausted, like a man who had run twenty miles to bring bad news. "They won't do anything to endanger it. Whatever they do to others, they won't hurt us."

"Maybe you should just put it down on the pavement and walk away," suggested Lys. "Let them handle it."

"No," said Randal. "I can't do that. They'd only try to use the statue for themselves, and it's too powerful for that—the evil in it has to be contained somehow, to keep it from doing any more harm."

*You know better than that,* said a voice in his mind. The old woman in his dream had spoken in just the same quiet, silken tones. *The magic is there for you, too.*

*Let me help you. Open yourself to me, and I will give you great power. I can save your life.*

"No!" Randal cried aloud. His two friends looked startled.

"What is it?" Lys asked, staring at Randal.

He shook his head. "Nothing. But let's get out of town as soon as we can."

"I'm with you on that," said Nick. "This hasn't exactly been the triumphant homecoming I planned on back when I was a boy." He pointed to where the opening of a side street made a darker blotch of shadow against the night. "If I remember right, that alley leads to a shortcut to the main gate."

"Have you thought about how we're going to convince the city guard to let us go?" Lys muttered.

"We'll worry about that when we get there," Nick answered as they turned the corner. Then the carpenter cursed under his breath as the three companions found themselves facing a blank wall. "Guess I remembered wrong," Nick said. "Looks like we'll have to retrace our steps a bit."

They started walking back toward the mouth of the alley. A red glow had begun to illuminate the underside of the clouds, and a smell of smoke came through the rain-swept air. *One of the lightning bolts must have started a fire,* thought Randal. From far away came the note of a bronze bell, sounding rapidly again and again.

He shook his head. "Fire, Lord Fess's men, the city guard—how many of those others in the black robes can still be left after all that?"

"Just three of us," came a voice from the mouth of

the alley. Three hooded and robed figures stepped into the gap between the walls, blocking off all escape.

"We are the only ones to escape from the yellow riders and the city guard," said the one who had spoken, "but I am the master, and two of my acolytes are with me. And you—you are the only other wizard in this entire town. There is no need for us to fight each other. Give me the statue and you will go free. I guarantee it."

A harsh shout from behind the speaker interrupted him. "Like you guaranteed your payment to me, wizard—with gold that turned to rocks?"

"Dagon!" Nick shouted. The mercenary, still wearing his studded leather armor, his sword ready, had stepped out into the street behind the three hooded figures. Lightning flashed, and the blue light glittered from his blade.

"You betrayed me!" Dagon said to the hooded man.

"Why not?" The hooded man gave him a little bow. "You betrayed your own companions. See if they will take you back now, if you wish to share their fate."

"Don't mock me, wizard!" Dagon swung his sword against the tallest man.

The master wizard blocked with a gesture, and Dagon's sword rebounded from empty air, spitting sparks. But the mercenary didn't pause. He whirled and threw a blow against the acolyte to his left. At the same time, he glanced down the alley to where Randal and his friends stood.

"Run, you fools!" he shouted.

The three ran past where Dagon held the magicians at bay, and on down the street. The wind howled, and the rain came at them in horizontal sheets. When Randal could go no farther without pausing to rest, they stopped again and huddled for shelter behind a horse trough in front of a closed building. Lights showed in the cracks of the shutters above.

Another body appeared out of the downpour and thudded to a seat beside them against the trough.

"Dagon!" Lys exclaimed.

The mercenary was bleeding freely from a deep cut that ran from his left eyesocket down to his jaw. He didn't seem to notice the wound. "Who did you expect?" he asked Lys. "The High King?"

"Certainly not you," said Lys. "Not after the way you sold us out."

Dagon shrugged. "I was just taking care of myself. Who wouldn't?"

"*I* wouldn't," said Lys. "You get out of here."

"Be quiet, girl. I'm on your side. No one double-crosses me and lives."

Randal looked at him. "Suppose we said that, too?"

"Can you fight them?" demanded the mercenary. "They would have had you a hundred times by now, if it weren't for me slowing them down."

"If you aren't on their side, why haven't they blasted you with lightning yet?" Randal asked.

Dagon reached into a pocket and pulled out the

114

amulet he'd taken from Varnart's henchman. "So far this little toy has kept me safe."

"Those charms don't last forever," Nick said. "One of these times, the magic will get through, and then we'll have one headache less. Now get out of here. We don't want your help."

"You'll be sorry," said Dagon.

Nick stood, picked the mercenary up by the front of his leather jacket, and dropped him into the horse trough. "I'm sorry already," said the former apprentice. "Now get out of my sight before I become sorrier still." He turned back to Randal and Lys. "Come on. Let's go."

The three walked off, leaving Dagon spluttering in the water trough.

"What's that booming sound?" asked Lys, after they had gone a little farther.

"The sea on the cliffs," Nick answered. "We must have gotten turned around while we were running —we're heading back toward the port again."

Randal said nothing. He'd heard that hollow pounding noise before—during his dream in the prison cell. *The old woman led me up onto the seawall to die,* he thought. *Is she leading me there now?*

A lightning stroke hit close overhead, and thunder rang with an ear-aching boom. The glare of the lightning revealed three hooded shadows at the end of the street—the master wizard and his two acolytes, waiting motionless for Randal and his companions to come up to them.

*They're following the statue,* Randal thought. *They can tell where it is. This is it—we can't hide anymore.*

115

"Nick," he said. "Lys. Get away while you can—they'll go for me first, to get the statue."

"We'll stick together," said Nick. The former apprentice wizard halted and put a hand on Randal's shoulder. "Three against one are bad odds. You need another wizard on your side—if you release the binding spell the Schola put on me, I can fight them alongside you."

Randal looked down the street at the three who waited. They still hadn't moved—they just stood there, motionless. *Wherever I go, they'll find me.* "I'm only a journeyman," he protested to Nick. "How can I break a spell the Regents cast?"

A lightning bolt lit the street. Rain was streaming down Nick's face. "Make me your apprentice—give me your permission—I don't know. But I know you can do it somehow."

Randal bit his lip hard, tasting blood. He'd worked more magic tonight than he ever had before, and his own magical reserves were already almost empty. He knew that three against two made better odds—they might even have a chance that way.

"Yes," he said. "Use your magic and help me."

It was as if the simple words were a powerful spell. Randal felt the same mental snap that he did when he finished a complicated conjuration. *The binding spell must have been set to end if a wizard gave Nick permission to work magic,* thought Randal.

At the same moment, Nicolas straightened, as if a weight had fallen from his shoulders. "That's done it," he said with a laugh. "Thanks, Randy—it looks like I've come back home as a wizard after all."

116

The one-time carpenter turned and faced the three who stood at the end of the street. "No use waiting for them to start it," he said. He lifted his hand and began chanting.

Randal recognized the shock spell that Nick was speaking. He felt the magic build up and falter—Nick's skills had lain too long unused. Time and practice would bring them back to what they had once been, but Nick didn't have time. Just as Master Laerg had once done for him, Randal spoke the words of strengthening and steadying.

Nick threw the spell successfully, and one of the two hooded figures went down. At the same time, another figure broke away from the shadows between two buildings behind the hooded men and ran forward. The two cloaked and hooded ones cast a bolt of red fire. The other man, the one attacking from behind, cried in Dagon's voice, "By the moon and the stars, wizards—face me!"

Dagon swung his sword as he shouted, and one of the two hooded figures crumpled to the street. But the red fire had already found its target, and Nick fell, blasted backward, his body outlined in crimson light. Randal threw a fireball at the one remaining wizard, and then he and Lys sprinted for the spot where Nick lay.

They dragged him around the corner, with Lys taking one arm and Randal the other. *He's too hot and limp*, Randal thought, unwilling to look down for fear of what he might be forced to see.

As soon as they were out of sight of their enemies, they lowered Nick to the ground. Randal flung himself to his knees beside Nick's unmoving body, feeling desperately for any trace of a heartbeat in his friend's chest and finding none. He called out the words of one healing spell after another, drawing still deeper on his own depleted strength. Nothing worked.

At last Lys crouched beside him. "Randal," she called out over the sound of the driving rain. "You have to stop. He's dead, Randy—you can't do anything for him now."

# X.

# The City and the Sea

RANDAL KNELT, looking down at his friend's body, and felt colder and lonelier than he had ever felt in his life.

"Master Laerg was right," he whispered. "Being near me can be deadly."

*You caused this,* said the voice of the old woman from his dream, seeming to call out to him from the statue he carried. *You can still change it if you truly want to. Only take the power that I offer, and you can strike down the ones who killed your friend, or smash this whole city into rubble. . . .*

"Lies!" Randal cried out, his voice breaking. "All lies!"

*You could even bring him back.*

Randal pressed his clenched fist against his mouth. This time, he knew that the statue spoke the truth. The temptation to open himself to that limitless, tainted power pulled at him almost uncontrollably. For a long time the young wizard knelt on the wet cobblestones, fighting back the words that would undo all that had happened since he'd lifted the binding spell.

*I want my friend back,* he thought. *I don't want to have killed him. I could use the statue, and Nick would get up from the street right now. But he wouldn't be the same man that I knew before. There are some things that should never be done, no matter what the reason, and calling the dead back to life is one of them.*

Still he did not move away from where Nick lay silent on the cobblestones. At last Lys pulled Randal to his feet. Tears ran freely down her cheeks, and her voice had lost all its music as she said again, "There's nothing you can do for him, Randy—we have to run."

He hesitated until finally Lys dragged him away— and still he looked backward, stumbling as he ran, until Nick's body was out of sight behind them.

After that, Randal lost track of time and place, following where Lys led without caring where they went. The storm raged all around them, and cold water ran in the streets. Then the booming noise of the sea rose up again out of the darkness, louder and nearer than before. Lys halted and laid a hand on his arm.

"Randal," she said, "stick by me. We'll head for the seawall and try to find the port gate from there."

He ran on a little longer, following the lute-player's slender figure in and out of the shadows. The street turned into a series of stone steps, worn with use and slick with the driving rain. Randal mounted the steps and found himself on the city wall overlooking the ocean—a place he had been before only in a dream. He turned to Lys, but his friend was nowhere in sight.

"Lys? Lys!" he cried, but his voice hardly carried above the sound of the wind. He was alone on the rainswept height.

Then he heard the sound of laughter. "Give me the statue now. Or you will meet the same fate as your friends."

The tall, black-hooded master wizard stood before Randal, blocking his path back down to the city. Behind the journeyman, the sea beat against the shattered rocks below. He had nowhere to retreat.

Randal looked around him. Lys was gone. The city walls were empty. The cold rain soaked his garments to his body, and deep, bone-numbing fatigue crushed down on him. The statue in the bag seemed the only real thing in the universe. And Randal's enemy stood before him, too strong and cruel for him to fight.

Randal stripped the leather bag away. The old woman looked at him, her face turned up in the darkness toward his.

"Is this what you want?" Randal called to the man who faced him. He held up the statue. "It is death and all the hateful things in the world."

"I know," the master wizard replied. "But it is power. Give it to me." He took a step forward.

Randal turned. The sea boomed below him. White spray flew up from the rocks, and the violent wind sent it whipping above the edge of the wall. Even the guards had hidden from the storm—no one was there to see anything that would happen.

*You dreamed this. You know what to do,* whispered a little voice at the back of his mind.

121

The master wizard of Widsegard walked slowly up the steps onto the seawall. His long, hooded robe swirled about him as he ascended. Randal cradled the statue in his arms and watched as the man approached.

Then Randal was aware of another man at his own shoulder—one tall and fair-haired, with embroidered robes semi-transparent in the fitful illumination of the lightning.

"Master Laerg!" Randal cried out. "Have you come to watch me die, then?"

"No, Randal," Laerg answered. "I've come to help you."

Randal shook his head. "I don't trust you."

"I suppose I deserve that," said the ghost. "But I tell you, I am more your friend than he is." Laerg pointed with a misty finger at the black-robed wizard.

Randal followed the ghost's gesture and looked at the sorcerer. He was frozen in mid-step. The sea had halted, and the rain no longer fell, but the air was full of drops hanging suspended between the clouds and the ground. The sound of the storm had quieted; Master Laerg and Randal stood inside an enormous circle of silence.

"What's happening?" Randal asked, curious. An eerie calmness filled him, as though all emotion had been washed out of him by the driving wind and rain.

"You are outside time, now," Laerg replied. "I am outside of time more often than in it, since that morning in Tarnsberg. Now you are close to joining me. Can't you feel it?"

Randal thought of how nice it would be to lie down and go to sleep, to not wake up, to rest. So many times tonight, only Nick or Lys pulling him along had kept him from sinking into that warm darkness.

"Yes," he said. "I feel it. Does that make you happy?"

"It would be very easy for you to join me," the ghost replied. "But I must ask you not to. There is something else that you need to do."

"What is it?"

Laerg shook his head, a smile on his semi-transparent features. "I'm sorry, but I can't tell you. I'm not sure myself, only that you have a task yet to perform in the world."

"But what am I to do *now?*" Randal cried.

"That's obvious," said the ghost. "Destroy that statue."

"But it's an artifact of power," protested Randal. "Its magical energy is huge. Once it is destroyed, all that energy will be lost forever. I can't do that."

"Yes, you can," said Laerg with a hint of his old arrogant impatience. "The statue is playing you false. Just as it draws you and gives you power, it is drawing and empowering your enemy. See, even now, he is draining the magical power that you hold, taking from you so that he himself may grow stronger. Where do you think this master wizard has gotten all the energy he has used this night?

"Just break the statue and let it be gone. Don't worry about the loss of magic, there is magic enough in the world."

Laerg vanished.

Once more the sea boomed, the wind howled, and the raindrops stung Randal's cheeks.

The master wizard of Widsegard reached the top of the stairs and stepped out onto the seawall. He stretched out his hand, and Randal started to turn and run. Then he saw that another, smaller person walked beside the master wizard. *Lys!*

"Lys!" Randal cried aloud. "Lys! Get away! Run!"

The wizard chuckled. "No, she is one of mine. You should be happy that she is willing to die in your place."

Lys took a step closer to the edge of the wall. Spray from the breaking waves down below shot up into the air above her head. Randal remembered his dream, how the statue had called on him to jump into that very sea.

"No!" Randal shouted again. Another few steps, and Lys would be poised at the edge of the sea. He leaped forward and stood blocking her path. The cold spray cascaded over him, and he could feel the wind blowing up from the abyss at his back.

"Have it as you will," said the master wizard, and called a flaming sword to his hand. Randal could feel his energy sinking lower as the blade appeared. The weapon burned with a clear red light and shot painful beams into Randal's eyes. The master wizard lifted his blade to strike.

"Your strength is fading," said the master wizard to Randal, "even as mine grows." He swept downward with the sword.

Randal pushed Lys out of the way with all his

strength and then blocked the blow with the only defense he had—the ivory statue in his left hand. The sword of flame struck and rebounded off the piece of carved ivory. But the shock of the impact drove Randal down onto his knees.

Burning pain filled his hand like a swarm of wasps stinging him all at once. He knew that a second blow would make him drop the statue, and the third would kill him.

Above him, the master wizard laughed. "You will die, the statue will be mine, and the city will know the true meaning of magic," he said. "Die then, you and the girl together."

The master wizard stepped forward, flaming sword upraised.

Randal tried to summon a magical weapon of his own—and failed. The dark place within him where he had found power before, from which he had drawn the reserves he hadn't known he possessed, was empty.

And the sweet whisper in his mind came and said, *Now you have no choice. You are mine, and you must come to me.*

"No," said Randal aloud. "I will not. No." Still the whisper of power went on in his mind: *Come to me, use me, you have no choice.* Resolutely, he closed his ears to the tempting voice. "There is magic enough in the world," he said. He put the piece of brittle ivory against his knee and broke it in two.

The broken statue twisted and writhed in his hands like a living thing. The master wizard's flaming sword burst into a huge flare as the power of

125

the statue escaped into the world, turning the blade's wielder into a human torch. The wizard staggered forward, tottered off the edge of the city wall, and fell, flaming, all the way into the sea so far below.

Randal staggered to his feet. Around him, streaks of blue and purple lightning flashed down from the gray, cloud-filled sky, and return streaks rose back from earth and sea to strike the clouds again. The noise of thunder came like the sound of mountains splitting in two. The wind howled. And in the driving rain, Randal saw ghosts.

Master Laerg stood at his side. The wild wind whipped through his old teacher's golden hair. "You have done well. The only correct choice."

Nick came up to him and embraced him. "I'm so proud of you, Randy. You saved the day for everyone."

Randal hugged him back, weeping unashamedly. "Oh, Nick, I'm so glad to see you. I thought you were dead."

"I am." The solid flesh of Nick's arm became air as the dead man spoke. "But Lys is alive. You have to help her."

"She's here," said Randal. "I have her safe."

"No, Randy," said Nick. "Lys isn't here."

Randal looked over at the girl he had pulled from the wall and recoiled in horror. This was the old woman, the statue full size and brought to life, and now she stirred and stood upright.

"Come with me," she said.

Randal turned and ran down the steps toward the street. He could hear the old woman's slow footsteps following behind him as he ran. He ran through the

streets of Widsegard, and always the footsteps and the tap-tap-tap of her staff sounded close behind him. No matter how fast he ran, every time he stopped for breath her dragging footsteps had drawn a little nearer.

When he tripped on a wet stone and fell to his knees, he knew he could run no farther. He knelt, sobbing, while the noise of the footsteps and the staff filled his ears.

"Come with me," a girl's voice said. The voice of his dream. He looked up. It was Lys.

He put out a hand to touch her. "Where did you come from? Are you alive?"

"Are you?" she asked. "Does it matter? Come with me."

Randal got to his feet and stumbled after her. Another hand took him by the other arm and helped him forward—this hand belonged to a muscular arm in studded leather. It was Dagon, battered and bleeding from his wounds but still upright.

"Move out," the mercenary said.

A tremor ran through the paving stones under their feet. Lightning played over the towers and battlements of the city. The crashing of the waves increased, even though Randal and his companions were running away from the sea. A wall collapsed in front of them, and they fled down another way. All around them, the ground heaved and shivered.

They reached the Great Gate—and found it blocked by an entire troop of city guards.

"We're all dead," said Lys. "They'll never let us past."

"Well, it wasn't a long life, but I had fun," Dagon said with a chuckle. He loosened his sword in the scabbard.

"Onward, then," Randal said. He had to hold on to Dagon and Lys so that he could stand at all.

Then the Great Gate collapsed, and the walls with it, while the wind roared around them and cold water ran ankle-deep in the streets. A mob of men and women surged through the main plaza of Widsegard, driven out of the crumbling buildings by the earthquake. The three companions were pushed and shoved and almost separated by the crowd, but still they moved forward.

A low moaning noise arose from the mass of people in the plaza—the sound of fear even greater than anything the storm and earthquake could bring. Randal looked up. The crushing black of the night was illuminated by the internal glow of the gigantic figure of an old woman, striding down from the hills of the Wilderness of Lannad, coming toward the gates of the city.

"I have to go face her," said Randal. He was too tired to feel anything except a kind of resignation, as though his long journey was at its unavoidable end. "There's no other wizard in the city now but me."

"You'll get killed," Dagon pointed out reasonably.

"I think I'm dead already," Randal said, feeling weary to his bones. "But it doesn't matter. Somebody has to stop her, or the entire city will perish."

"Then I'll go with you," said Lys.

"So will I," said Dagon. The mercenary laughed. "You might say I started this. I want to see the end."

"No," said Randal. He pulled away from them. "One friend died for me already tonight. No more."

Randal pushed his way through the wailing crowd, past men in yellow surcoats who never turned to stop him, past guardsmen who had eyes only for the death that came striding down upon Widsegard. Step by step, while the earth rocked and the wind shrieked around him, he mounted the rubble of the city walls. There he stood, facing the old woman one more time as she came toward the city in slow steps that spanned a league or more at every stride.

*It can't be real. It doesn't really exist.*

The thing came closer.

*If I'm killed by unreal things, am I really dead?*

"Yes, you are," said Nick from beside him. His friend's features were faint and transparent against a sky full of blue-black clouds.

"Not that there's anything wrong with being dead," said Laerg's ghost from his other side. "Eventually you will be, like it or not."

"But not now!" Randal cried. He gathered what remained of his powers to him, and nothing answered. He was as empty of magic as a broken bowl. *There's nothing left of me. I've used it all, and there's nothing left to stop death from taking the entire city.*

He looked back over his shoulder at the city behind him. Everything appeared far away and very pale. The mass of people crowding the ruined streets had blurred and faded until he couldn't make out the invididual figures at all. Only the ghosts seemed real—the ghosts and the old woman.

*Why am I seeing the dead more clearly than the living tonight?* he wondered, and turned back to the semi-transparent figures beside him. "Master Laerg, Nick—what do you want me to do?"

"Save the city," Nick told him. "Put an end to the evil magic before everything is destroyed."

"I can't," said Randal. He wept at his own helplessness and felt the hot tears sting his cheeks. "My strength is gone. There's nothing left."

"You have us," Master Laerg replied. "We helped to make you what you are, and we are a part of you forever. Let us help you now."

Randal looked from one ghostly form to the other—the teacher he had killed, the friend who had died trying to save him. "Stand beside me, then," he said. "Give me the strength to defeat this magic. Say the spell with me."

He began the words of the spell of dismissal. "*Vanesce*," he called out in the Old Tongue. "*Fuge* . . ."

As he cast the spell he drew on the power of the ghostly wizards who stood beside him, using their magical energy as if it were his own. Laerg had the deep reserves of a master of the Art, and an almost dizzying strength. Nick was only an apprentice, but his lesser power was clear and bright, untouched by the shadows that clouded Laerg.

Randal chanted on, letting the magical energy flow through him into the words of the spell. On his right and his left the two other wizards chanted along with him. He gestured and saw the two beside him echo the movement. *Now for the end,* he thought, and pulled in all the power that he could find.

Neither Laerg nor Nick would have anything left now, nor would they be able to reappear in the world—Randal was draining them to the very last of their reserves—but they gave their strength to him freely.

"*Redi ad umbras, figura mortis!*" Randal shouted, and directed the whole force of the spell at the monstrous apparition looming above him.

The old woman faltered, then slowed. Finally, her footsteps halted at the very outskirts of the city. Her image thinned out against the stormy sky and then drifted away like fragments of a cloud, with no more sound to mark her going than the keening of the wind. The ghosts vanished, and their magic drained out of Randal, leaving him even emptier than before.

*It's finally over,* thought Randal. *I can rest now.* He sank to the stone under his feet, and into a sleep deeper than he had ever known.

How long he slept, Randal never knew. At first, he didn't even dream. Then there were nightmares, and voices talking someplace near, and after that, undisturbed rest again. When he finally awoke, he was lying on his back and looking up at green branches, with warm sunlight dappling down through the leaves overhead.

Randal turned his head—there was a pillow under it, and a pallet under him—and he realized that he had not collapsed here, but had been brought here and cared for in this sunny place that smelled of life and morning. He stretched, testing his strength, and sat up.

He saw that he was in an olive grove, on a patch of high ground not far from Widsegard. The hillside sloped away toward the sea, and the towers and rooftops of the great city clustered around the water in the distance.

A few feet away, Lys sat with her back against a tree, singing in a quiet voice. She didn't have her lute but sang without accompaniment:

> "Blow up the fire, my maidens,
> Bring water from the well,
> For all my house shall feast this night
> Now that my sons are well."

Randal looked within himself once more. He had magical energy again, more and purer than he had ever known. He whispered the words that called up the spell of sound, to accompany Lys since she had no instrument of her own. She heard the music and turned to face him. "Welcome back," she said.

"I was afraid you were lost," Randal said. "I think I dreamed it. You were lost, and Nick was dead, and the whole city was destroyed. . . . I can't tell where the truth stopped and the dream began."

Lys gave a shaky laugh. "The city's as whole as it ever was, or so I hear—a bit of damage down by the port, and a couple of buildings lost to a lightning fire, but nothing you wouldn't expect from a bad storm."

Randal gave a sigh of relief. *I never wanted to tear down an entire city, not even to destroy something as evil as that statue.* He paused a moment. "And . . . Nick?"

Lys bent her head. "No, that part wasn't a dream. He's really gone."

Randal closed his eyes to stop the tears that threatened to spill down over his cheeks. When he had his voice back under control, he asked, "What happened to you at the end?"

She shook her head. "All I remember is following you through the streets, and then you were gone. I figured out later that I'd been following an illusion."

"An illusion must have been leading me as well," said Randal. "I thought that you were with me and never noticed that we'd been separated."

"What was that statue, anyway," asked Lys, "that it could cause so much trouble and destruction?"

"An artifact of power," said Randal. "Very old and very strong. Whoever made it, long ago, never meant it for anything good . . . and over the years it grew stronger and more wicked, full of the magical energy it took from the wizards it killed. In the end," he finished with a shudder, "the statue became almost like Death itself. I don't think anybody could have controlled it."

"Why did it bring us here?"

"The statue was made in Widsegard," Randal said. "The city was its home, and the place of its greatest strength. If its power had gone unchecked, it might have continued drawing energy into itself until all the world was drained dry."

Lys's dark blue eyes were almost black with remembered fear. "Was that what those wizards in the city wanted to see happen—the death of everything?"

Randal shook his head wearily. "I don't think so. They wanted the power a magical artifact can give, so they tried to call the statue to them . . . and the statue was only too glad to answer. It worked on Varnart until he hired Dagon and Bryce to steal it from Lord Fess's treasury. But Varnart would have kept the statue in Brecelande, so it killed Bryce and came to me. And I—almost—brought it the rest of the way."

He bowed his head for a moment, thinking of that last struggle on the walls of the city. How much had been real, and how much only nightmare, he would probably never know. *It doesn't matter anyway,* he realized. *Wizards fight their battles in a realm where dreams and reality are one. If I'd held back from facing the old woman, I would have awakened to find all of Widsegard leveled by storm and fire, and the statue lying unbroken in the rubble.*

He sat in silence for a minute or two, while the salt breeze off the sea stirred the leaves in the olive grove. After a while, Randal heard the sound of footsteps coming up the hill and turned.

A man was climbing into the grove. "Dagon!" Randal said. "Of all the people I didn't want to see . . ."

"Don't judge him too harshly," Lys said. "After the storm was over, he helped me get you out of Widsegard and up here where we could hide out from the guard and Fess's men."

"They were still looking for you then," Dagon explained, coming up beside Randal and sitting down cross-legged on the ground. "That bunch of wizards, though—they're gone for good, as far as anyone can tell. But that's old news, and I came up here with fresh, for a change."

Randal looked at the mercenary suspiciously. "You bought back your lucky dagger?"

Dagon shook his head. "I never thought you'd hold a man's mistakes against him, wizard. No, I've joined the city guard. There's been quite a shakeup lately in town, and they were recruiting. I thought you'd enjoy the joke of it—my nightmare's come true, and I've taken an honest job."

Randal regarded the older man for a moment longer, then smiled faintly in spite of himself. "More or less honest," he said, and Dagon laughed.

"Dagon's been taking good care of us," Lys told Randal, "ever since he and I found you on the seawall with that statue broken in your hands."

"So I did break it," said Randal. "That much was real, then. What did you do with the pieces?"

"Took the girl's advice," Dagon replied, "and threw them into the ocean."

"Thank you," said Randal to the mercenary. "I think I came closer to death—in several ways—because of that statue than I want to be again. And I don't think I could have made it back without your help."

Dagon actually looked somewhat shamefaced, as if gratitude were something new to his experience. "You were shouting all kinds of nonsense," he said. "And you've been out for days. This is the first time I've seen you awake since then." He paused. "Are the two of you going to be moving along soon?"

Lys tilted her head curiously. "Should we be thinking about it?"

136

"Well," said Dagon, "wizardry's still outlawed in the city, and the city guard has a warrant for your friend there. Sooner or later, somebody's going to notice that you're up here and think about sending out a troop, just to make an arrest and keep things tidy."

"How long do you think we have?" Randal asked.

"Long enough to get you back on your feet," said Dagon. "But probably not much more than that. And I'd start figuring out which way you want to head, just in case you have to get going in a hurry."

"We can't go back to the north," Randal said. "Master Varnart and Lord Fess are up there, and neither one is likely to feel kindly toward me after what I did to that statue."

"We could go south," Lys said. "That's where I come from, and we'll be beyond any borders that Brecelande ever claimed."

"South," said Randal. He recalled the spices and fruits that had come into Widsegard from the southern trade. The thought called up images of warmth and light, new places without old memories to darken them, new learning, even new magic.

"Yes," he said. "We'll go south."

*Read the first exciting book in the series*

# CIRCLE OF MAGIC ❶

## SCHOOL OF WIZARDRY

by Debra Doyle and James D. Macdonald

**Randal thought he wanted to be a wizard . . .**

As a young squire, Randal seems assured of a future as a knight—until a mysterious wizard enters the castle gates.

To his astonishment, Randal discovers that he himself possesses special powers. He leaves the security of life as a squire to become a student at the School of Wizardry.

Once his training in the mystic arts has begun, however, Randal soon learns that there are many perils—and one deadly enemy—to be overcome before he can advance from sorcerer's apprentice to journeyman wizard. . . .

ISBN 0-8167-6936-2

*Available wherever you buy books.*

*Read the second exciting book in the series*

# CIRCLE OF MAGIC ❷

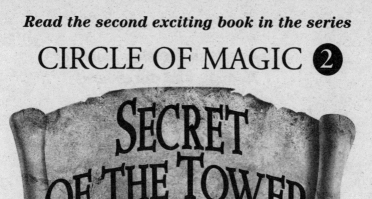

## SECRET OF THE TOWER

by Debra Doyle and James D. Macdonald

### What's a wizard without magic?

Randal broke his promise—the vow that all apprentice wizards must take never to use a weapon. Now Randal can graduate from the School of Wizardry only on one condition: that he not use magic until he is pardoned by a master wizard.

Randal must travel to the wizard's faraway tower . . . a journey made all the more perilous because he may use neither sword nor magic for protection.

When Randal finally reaches the mysterious tower, it appears to be abandoned. But he soon discovers that the building holds a deadly secret . . .

ISBN 0-8167-6937-0

*Available wherever you buy books.*

*Read the next exciting book in the series*

# CIRCLE OF MAGIC 4

## DANGER IN THE PALACE

by Debra Doyle and James D. Macdonald

### Friend or foe?

When Randal and his best friend, Lys, are invited to join the theater troupe in the court of a kind and wealthy prince, they think they have it made!

But Randal soon stumbles upon a plot against the prince and discovers that his wizardry skills are needed now more than ever.

Can Randal expose the prince's enemies before it's too late?

ISBN 0-8167-6939-7

*Available wherever you buy books.*